STORIES FOR LATE NIGHT DRINKERS

INTERMEDIA

STORIES FOR LATE NIGHT DRINKERS

Michel Tremblay

Translated by
Michael Bullock

Intermedia
Vancouver

Second printing, 1979

Third printing, 1980

ACKNOWLEDGEMENT

is due to the Editor of *The Canadian Fiction Magazine*, in whose pages some of these translations first appeared.

Original French edition, *Contes Pour Buveurs Attardés*, first published in 1966. Copyright © 1966 by Editions du Jour.

Tremblay, Michel, 1943-
[Contes pour buveurs attardés. English]
Stories for late night drinkers

Translation of Contes pour buveurs attardés.
ISBN 0-88956-055-2

I. Title. II. Title: Contes pour buveurs attardés.
PS8539.R44C613   C843'.5'4   C77-002219-7
PR9199.3

ISBN No. 0-88956-055-2, paper

Stories for Late Night Drinkers was designed and printed by Intermedia Press, Box 3294, Vancouver, B.C., Canada V6B 3X9.

TABLE OF CONTENTS

For André Brassard
For Guy Bergeron

PART ONE
Stories Told By Drinkers

FIRST DRINKER:
THE HANGED MAN

In my country, when someone kills his neighbour they hang him. It's stupid, but that's the way it is. It's in the laws.

My job is to watch over the hanged. In the prison where I work, a hanged man isn't taken down as soon as he is dead. No, he is left hanging all night and it's my job to watch over him until sunrise.

I'm not required to weep, but I do weep all the same.

*   *   *

I knew very well this hanged man wasn't going to be an ordinary hanged man. Unlike all the condemned men I had seen up to then, this one didn't seem to be afraid. He didn't smile, but his eyes didn't betray any fear. He looked at the gallows coldly,

whereas the other condemned men almost unfailing-
ly go into shock when they see it. Yes, I felt that this
hanged man wouldn't be an ordinary hanged man.

*   *   *

When the trapdoor opened and the rope stretched taut with a dry sound, I felt something move in
my belly.

The hanged man didn't struggle. All those I had
seen till this one had twisted about, swinging at the
end of the rope with their knees drawn up. But this
one didn't move.

He didn't die immediately. You could hear him
trying to breathe . . . . But he didn't move. He didn't
move at all. We looked at each other, the hangman,
the prison governor and I, wrinkling our foreheads.
This lasted a few minutes; then, suddenly, the
hanged man let out a long yell that sounded to me
like the huge laughter of a madman. The hangman
said that was the end.

The hanged man quivered. His body seemed to
lengthen a little. Then, nothing more.

But I was sure he had laughed.

*   *   *

I was alone with the hanged man who had laughed. I couldn't stop myself from looking at him. He
seemed to have grown longer still. And that hood I
have always hated! That hood which hides everything but lets you imagine everything! I never see
the faces of the hanged, but I guess what they're like
and I think that's even worse.

All the lights had been put out and the little
nightlight over the door had been lit.

How black it was and how afraid I was of this hanged man.

In spite of myself, around two in the morning, I dozed off. I was woken—I couldn't say just when—by a low sound, like a sigh. Was it me who had sighed like that? It must have been me, I was alone. I had probably sighed in my sleep and my sigh had woken me.

Instinctively, I turned my eyes towards the hanged man. He had moved! He had made a quarter turn and now he was facing me. It wasn't the first time this had happened. It was due to the rope, I knew that perfectly well. But all the same I couldn't help trembling. And that sigh. That sigh which I wasn't certain had come out of my mouth.

I called myself a double-dyed idiot and got up to walk around a bit. As soon as I had turned my back on the hanged man, I heard the sigh again. I was quite sure this time that it wasn't me who had sighed. I didn't dare turn round. I felt my legs turn to water and my throat dry up. I heard two or three more sighs, which soon changed into breathing, first very uneven, then more regular. I was absolutely certain the hanged man was breathing and I thought I was going to faint.

At last I turned round, trembling all over. The dead man was moving. He was swinging, almost imperceptibly, at the end of his rope. And he was breathing more and more strongly. I got as far away from him as I could, taking refuge in a corner of the big room.

I shall never forget the horrible spectacle that followed. The hanged man had been breathing for about five minutes, when he started to laugh. He suddenly stopped breathing loudly and began to laugh softly. It wasn't a demoniacal, or even a cynical, laugh; it was simply the laugh of someone who is wildly amused. His laughter quickly grew louder and soon the hanged man was roaring with laughter, fit to burst his sides. He was swinging more and more violently . . . laughing . . . laughing . . .

I was sitting on the ground, my two arms squeezed to my stomach, and I was crying.

The dead man was swinging so violently that at one moment his feet almost touched the ceiling. This went on for several minutes. Minutes of pure terror for me. Suddenly the rope broke and I let out a loud cry. The hanged man hit the ground with a thud. His head came off and rolled over to my feet. I jumped up and ran for the door.

*   *   *

When the caretaker, the prison governor and I returned to the room, the body was still there, stretched out in a corner; but we couldn't find the dead man's head. It was never found.

SECOND DRINKER: CIRCE

I who am speaking to you have ploughed the seas and been to countless different countries. I've even seen a country that perhaps doesn't exist. That's as true as I'm sitting here. You don't believe me? Listen . . . .

We had set sail from Liverpool one 24th of June and were making for . . . I don't remember exactly which port we were headed for. Anyway, it was the 29th of June and it was hot. I had chosen the evening watch because I like to see the sun disappear into the sea. Every evening, around half past eight, I used to settle down at the bow of the ship, just behind the figure-head that represented a mermaid with golden hair and inviting breasts, and watch the sun shrink, go down into the sea and then disappear completely. Once the last rays of the sun had disappeared I used to look at the mermaid and . . . It's silly, but I used to have the impression that the two of us were feeling the same thing. A kind of nostalgia, a kind of tightening of the throat . . . well.

Then I would go back to my post and it used to take me at least three or four pipes to calm down again.

Well, it was the evening of the 29th of June. The heat had been overpowering all day long and the sea was as flat as the palm of a nun's hand. I was leaning over the rails quietly smoking a pipe, waiting to see the sun go down. I was alone on the bridge. I stress this because later I tried to find someone who might also have witnessed what happened, but I never found anyone and everyone said I had been dreaming. But do people dream with their eyes open? I'm not a poet and when I see and hear things, I see them and hear them!

The sea was orange and the sun was almost touching it when I heard a distant voice. It was as though a woman were singing away in the west. I looked up at the sky, but there were no birds. Anyhow, seabirds don't sing like that. It really was a woman's voice. A languorous voice, a voice that took you by the entrails and told you things without even uttering words. I had just taken up a position below the figure-head and I raised my telescope. Far away, just alongside the sun, there was an island. I knew quite well there was no island in this part of the ocean and that we shouldn't see land for another three or four days . . . I almost shouted "Land ho!", but something prevented me. I think it was the voice that prevented me from shouting.

No, don't laugh and listen to what followed.

The island seemed to be quite big and, surprisingly, it seemed to be moving. That's to say, after a few seconds I noticed that it was approaching our ship a bit too fast. Our ship couldn't be doing more than fifteen knots and the island was approaching at —well, let's say thirty or forty knots.

I was frightened, but the woman's voice, the woman's voice I could hear more and more distinctly, conveyed some peace to my soul. I don't know how to put it—it calmed me down or something. And I wanted to see who was singing like that.

When the island was quite close to the ship I saw in a small cove . . . Listen, you mustn't think I'm mad. I can swear that I really saw this creature. I wasn't dreaming. In a little cove, sitting on a rock level with the surface of the water, I saw our ship's mermaid, our beautiful figure-head, and she was singing and smiling and thrusting out her breasts to me. She was beautiful. If you had only seen her. She was gently squeezing her breasts and seemed to be inviting me to leave the ship and follow her I don't know where—perhaps to her country, to her world that isn't like ours, a world in which the women are always singing, always singing and smiling at you . . . Excuse me, every time I tell this story I can't help being moved. This country of song and happiness only appeared to me once, as the sun was setting; it only lasted a few seconds, but it caused me such pain. You see . . . No, you wouldn't understand. Forgive me.

THIRD DRINKER:
SIDI BEL ABBES BEN BECAR

I should like to tell you the story of Sidi bel Abbes ben Becar, the Arab who had discovered how to fertilize deserts. But before he died he made me swear never to disclose anything about his life or his secrets, and I must remain silent. But all the same, before leaving for distant seas, I should like to tell you that when you see giant trees laden with fruit growing in the middle of the desert, when you see the deserts themselves disappear forever, then you can dance and sing: "Hallelujah, Sidi bel Abbes ben Becar has come back." That's all I can tell you, but believe me, Sidi bel Abbes ben Becar will come back; he told me so.

FOURTH DRINKER: THE EYE OF THE IDOL

I have only recently returned from that far-off country called Paganka, where the blue men hunt the terrible hyena-bird, an enormous and terrifying monster that attacks the flocks and sometimes even humans; and where the women never cut their hair.

I had crossed half the earth before reaching that accursed country. After a very difficult journey lasting four months across savannahs and forests I finally came to Keabour, the capital of the country, situated in the midst of virgin forest. To tell the truth, Keabour is not even a town but at most a village of four or five hundred inhabitants, where the most rudimentary commodities and the most elementary laws of decency are still unknown. What struck me most on arriving in Keabour was the strange appearance of the blue women.

There is no more astonishing sight than these blue females with their long mop of hair, who look more like tangled spindles than women. The oldest drag behind them hair several feet long which they never wash and which ends up looking like dry dung.

After arriving in Keabour, I enquired as to the whereabouts of the temple of M'ghara, the aim of my journey. But no one seemed to know. However, M'ghara is the god of the country and I had often heard tell of the loathsome sacrifices offered to him in the temple by the inhabitants of Paganka. People even talked about human sacrifices, but nothing had ever been proved.

After three days I finally discovered an old man who, for a few bottles of liquor, agreed to sell me the secret of his people, on the grounds that he was not risking much because he was very old and was going to die in any case. It is a fact that death was the punishment for revealing the secret of the location of the temple of M'ghara. At least that is what the old man told me and I saw later that he had not been lying.

So I set out next day at dawn, mounted on a mule, in the direction of the Mountain With No Summit that can be seen from Keabour. The journey was very difficult because I had to hide every time I met an inhabitant of the country and also because of the ferocious beasts, the reptiles and the voracious insects that populate the jungle.

During the fourth night of my journey towards the Mountain With No Summit I was woken by the sound of a tom-tom very close by. I did not sleep for the rest of the night and the tom-tom did not stop until sunrise.

That day I reached the temple of M'ghara.

*   *   *

In the centre of a clearing rose a very ugly building that looked like a beehive and was built of a material which I recognized as graft, a brownish metal much used by the inhabitants of Paganka but of absolutely no value. I was very disappointed by the poverty-stricken appearance of the temple of M'ghara. Had I travelled across half the globe and risked my life countless times in order to discover such a wretched looking temple? I approached the building with chagrin and ascended the few steps leading to the portico. I was about to enter when I was startled by a cry behind me.

An altar had been set up close to the temple and upon this altar were stretched the old man who had shown me the way and an old woman whose hair had been cut off. The old man was already dead, but the woman was still alive and even had the strength to groan. I went up to the altar and bent over the woman. She opened her eyes and began to yell when she saw me. "Accursed be thou, stranger," she cried. "You have reached your goal but see what has happened to my husband and me. Soon the hyena-birds will come to take us to M'ghara, the terrible god with the six arms. And all because of you. Supreme shame, my own children cut off my hair before all the inhabitants of Keabour and spat in my face and in my husband's face. The high priest himself thrust the knife into my husband's chest and he only left me alive so that I should see the hyena-birds coming. I am dying because of my husband's sacrilege, that is the law of Paganka. But I curse Paganka and its laws. I curse its inhabitants. And I curse you, who have come so far in order to seize the eye of the idol with the six arms. Many have come before you, but none have ever got so far. May the curse of M'ghara be upon you. Beware of the eye, it . . . " The old woman suddenly stopped speaking and her eyes were fixed upon a dot moving in the sky above us. "Already," she whispered. "They are already here." She closed her eyes and moved no more. The dot came closer and closer and when it was close enough for me to make out its shape, I saw that it was a bird with the head of a hyena that was making towards us croaking horribly. I ran to the temple and entered the portico. I saw with horror that the temple had no doors — doors are unknown in Paganka — and I hid behind one of the pillars of graft supporting the roof. From my hiding place I could see what was happening outside the

the temple without being seen.

After two or three minutes, the hyena-bird landed beside the altar and went up to the two bodies. It sniffed at them for a few moments, then it screeched. There was a flapping of wings and a second hyena-bird joined the first. For a long time they sniffed at the two bodies without making up their minds to seize them. Suddenly they both raised their heads at the same time and looked in my direction. They had certainly sensed my presence, because they approached the temple and mounted the steps. But they stopped in the portico and contented themselves with looking at me — from their present position they could see me easily. Something seemed to be preventing them from entering the temple and this saved me. After looking at me malevolently for several long minutes, they returned to the altar. Then they each seized a body and soared up into the sky. I heard the old woman cry out. I came out of the temple to watch the hyena-birds fly away. They disappeared behind a large rock on the Mountain With No Summit.

*   *   *

The idol was also made of graft. It was very old and almost falling in ruins. If I had not been so exhausted by the long journey and the many adventures that had happened to me before reaching the temple of M'ghara, I should have laughed at the ridiculous situation in which I found myself. I had crossed half the world to find an idol that had absolutely no value. I had spent my entire fortune—very small, it is true—in the hope of discovering an infinitely greater one and now found myself, after months of exertion and privation, before a kind of six-armed monster that wasn't worth ten cents, that was grimacing at me and seemed to be mocking my discomfiture.

I was completely discouraged. I sat down at the foot of the idol, rested my head on one of its knees and would have started crying like a girl if a thought had not suddenly crossed my mind.

The old woman who had just been carried off by the hyena-bird had talked about the "eye of the idol". She had said that I had come to get the "eye of the idol". I raised my head and looked at M'ghara's one eye. There was nothing special about it. As big as a fist, it seemed to be made of graft like the rest of the statue. So why should the woman have attached so much importance to it? Stirred by a vain hope, I rose and climbed up onto the statue's knee. Using its arms like a ladder, I climbed right up to M'ghara's head. I was very much afraid the idol might collapse under my weight, but something at the back of my mind told me it was worth risking my life one last time.

I sat on the idol's shoulder and began to examine the eye. I quickly saw that it was not really made of graft. A thick layer of this metal covered a material that seemed very hard. I scratched the surface of the eye and a few bits of metal came away. Then I had a very clear impression that something was going on inside the statue. I felt a sort of shiver run through the whole idol and one of its arms moved. I told myself that the idol was probably having difficulty supporting my weight and that this movement of the arm was not dangerous. So I continued scratching and at the end of five minutes the whole layer of graft had come off. I moved closer to the eye and almost choked with surprise and joy. I had before my eyes the biggest diamond you can imagine. Finer and bigger than any I had ever seen in my life. Two seconds later, my knife was out of my pocket and I was beginning to scratch around the eye to loosen it. But the idol began to tremble and I thought I heard a stifled groan coming from its metal entrails. I began to feel really afraid and started scratching even more vigorously so as to finish my task as quickly as possible. At the first blow of the knife, M'ghara's head moved from left to right and one of its arms stretched out towards the sky. I was seized with panic and struck the eye with all my strength. The idol doubled up and uttered a yell of pain. I almost slipped off M'ghara's shoulders, but I managed to put one arm round his neck and remained suspended, my body up against his chest. Then I noticed that the idol was breathing.

The idol stopped moving. I climbed up onto its shoulders again. The diamond was almost completely loosened and I told myself that one more well placed blow with the knife would free it. But I hesitated. Wouldn't the idol start groaning and struggling again? But had it really groaned? Had I really felt the beating of its heart, or had I been the victim of my imagination?

I suddenly raised my arm and drove the knife one more time into M'ghara's eye. As soon as the diamond was completely detached, the idol stood up straight and put two of its hands to the wound, crying out. Its head struck the roof of the temple and the jolt nearly made me fall. But I managed to hang on to a pendant M'ghara wore in his ear. The idol began running this way and that through the temple, knocking into the pillars, falling to its knees, rising again and starting to run madly around again, yelling. Suddenly, one of its arms seized me and threw me down on the ground at the foot of a pillar. Half dazed, I got up and ran from the temple.

I ran for several minutes and finally collapsed under a tree. After resting for a few moments, I decided to take out the diamond, which I had hidden under my shirt, and look at it. Oh, I shall always remember the horror of that fateful moment! When I plunged my hand into my shirt, I cried out with disgust. I took out from beneath my clothes a huge, bloody eye, a horrible, viscous thing, that looked at me through a trickle of coagulated blood.

FIFTH DRINKER: GERBLICHT'S WINE

Gerblicht was my friend. Or at least, he said he was my friend. He was a rather amusing man and his often very witty repartee used to entertain me greatly. He was as intelligent as he was ugly and he was the ugliest being I had ever come across. But his strange ideas sometimes scared me. And he knew that. Also he often used to horrify me with his diabolical schemes. He had a mania for inventing all sorts of tortures for small animals; a mania that exasperated me in the highest degree. So he often used to come and show me a new invention and torture either a mouse, a cat or a rabbit in front of me. I must admit that at such moments I really believed Gerblicht was mad. But he always looked at me in such an intelligent, such a sensible way that I was forced to admit that he was only cruel. With a very studied, very refined cruelty.

One day he came to show me how he had succeeded in making one of his white mice dance. Foreseeing a new torture for these poor little creatures, I asked him not to carry out the demonstration, on the pretext that I had a terrible headache. But Gerblicht was determined to show me his new invention and nothing in the world could stop him. So that day I had to undergo one of the worst experiences of my life (the worst next to the one I shall recount further on).

He had brought a rectangular box about one foot long, six inches wide and six inches high. This box was made of iron or a metal that looked like iron. It was set on top of a small gas-cooker. So that we could see what was happening inside the box, Gerblicht had made a hole in the top and put a pane of glass in it. Inside the box was a little white mouse to which Gerblicht had given a big piece of cheese. The poor creature was quietly nibbling at the cheese with no suspicion of the horrors awaiting it.

Gerblicht told me I was going to see the mouse dance. With a cruel smile at the corners of his lips, he struck a match and put it to the gas-cooker under the box. Then I understood. I told Gerblicht not to light the stove; I told him I wouldn't tolerate a little animal that had done no one any harm being made to suffer like that in my house. But Gerblicht lit the cooker just the same. I took refuge in the remotest corner of the room with the firm intention of not watching what was happening inside the box.

Five minutes passed without any result. Then, suddenly, I heard a low cry. Thinking I was hearing the mouse squeaking, I was about to cover my friend with insults, but when I turned round I saw that it was my friend who had cried out. He was bending over his little box and his hideous face was transformed by a violent joy. The cries I had heard were cries of triumph he was uttering as he looked into his box. "Come and look," he called out. "It's beginning to dance." Then, as happened every time Gerblicht carried out a demonstration in my house, I was seized by an irresistible desire to look inside the box. I didn't want to know what was happening in that damned box, but something stronger than my will drew me towards it. So I approached in spite of myself and leaned over the rectangular cage.

When I regained consciousness, I still had in my head the terrible squeaks of the mouse maddened by the white-hot iron, and I had a splitting headache. Gerblicht was at my bedside, laughing softly. "You aren't very tough," he said. "You passed out almost at once. You missed the best part. You should have seen it towards the end, when . . . " I begged him to stop because I felt a need for rest. Gerblicht looked at me with a smile. "Very well," he said. "I'm going. But let me tell you, I think you're very weak. Almost like a little animal."

I fell asleep and dreamed all night long of the mouse hopping from one wall of its box to the other, trying to escape from the horrible burns it suffered from all sides at once. No way out. No way of escape. Fire . . . fire . . . all the time . . . without respite . . . without end . . . fire everywhere.

*   *   *

I didn't see Gerblicht until some time later, at the opera. I was chatting with a friend when I heard someone call out to me joyfully. "Good evening," said Gerblicht. "I'm very pleased to see you. All the more so because I've just received something for you. A present from Germany." But Gerblicht refused to tell me what the present was. "Thursday, yes, on Thursday I shall come and see you with my present. I hope you will be able to appreciate it at its true value."

The following Thursday I waited all day for my friend Gerblicht. But he didn't come. Finally, intrigued and, I must admit, a bit worried, I decided to go to his place to see if perhaps he wasn't well. Gerblicht was not at home. His servant told me his master had been away since Tuesday and he didn't know where he had gone. More and more worried, I returned home with the idea of going to the police station the following evening if my friend had not turned up.

On Friday morning, around six o'clock, I was woken by Gerblicht himself. "I'm sorry I didn't come yesterday," he said. "But I had something very important to finish." I got up and invited him to have breakfast with me. We chatted about all sorts of things throughout the meal and I was very glad to see that my friend did not touch upon the subject of his last visit . . . the dancing mouse. He seemed to have completely forgotten it. After breakfast, Gerblicht told me he had brought his famous present from Germany. Then he took a tiny bottle of wine out of his pocket. "There's my gift," he cried gaily. "You are about to taste the very finest wine . . . " He poured out a glass of this wine and handed it to me. "Take it," he said. "You can tell me what you think of it."

Whoever said there are no such things as premonitions was wrong. There are. At that instant, as I was about to put the glass of wine to my lips, something happened in me that I could not exactly describe. It was like a warning. Something in my chest, like a pressure on my heart, caused me to withdraw the glass from my mouth. I looked at Gerblicht. His eyes were riveted on me. He was staring at my mouth and his own mouth was half open as though he wanted to drink himself or to impel me to drink.

I knew I shouldn't drink that wine.

But I drank just the same.

It started in my throat. It was like a serpent of fire running down my throat. I tried to cry out, but no sound came from my mouth. And I began to fall. At the same time as the pain spread through my entire body, I felt myself falling. A fall in slow motion. Like in dreams, when you feel you are being pursued and are incapable of running. The more I fell the more intense became the pain. In my fall I had the impression of holding a bottle of wine and drinking it non-stop.

Suddenly, a stentorian voice filled the sky of my dream. "How do you like my wine? How do you like my wine?" said the voice. "It's good, isn't it?" An enormous laugh caused my bottle to break in pieces and I raised my arms to the sky. I was no longer falling. I was on a very white road. The ground was covered with whitish dust and an odour of decay filled the air. I was thirsty with a terrible, an unbearable thirst, a thirst such as I had never felt before. I absolutely had to drink. Absolutely!

A little man in rags came up to me and offered me a cup full of milk. I took the cup, but when I saw the man's face my stomach heaved and I couldn't drink. He had no eyelids!

He looked at me with his over-large eyes and seemed to be asking for something. I don't know what. He also seemed to be terribly tired. He was trembling with fatigue, and his hands, resting on his thighs, were shivering and seemed to be trying to break loose from his body in order to run away. I asked the man why he looked so tired. He told me with a groan that he hadn't slept for years because he no longer had any eyelids. "How can you rest when you have no eyelids?" he cried. "I suffer atrociously and shall never know rest. I shall never rest again because my eyes are forever open!" His eyes were full of the white dust that covered everything in that region. Then I told the man that I could perhaps save him. "Take my eyelids," I cried. "Take them, they're yours." But the man had disappeared.

"How do you like my wine? How do you like my wine?"

I was walking along the powdery road. Every time I put my foot on the ground, a cloud of dust rose all around me. I wasn't afraid. No, really, I wasn't afraid. But I was thirsty. Great trees of salt had grown up in the dusty plain and stood motionless in spite of the strong breeze.

And this voice that went on and on shouting.

I saw the strangest of men approaching me. He was terrifyingly thin and agitated by a constant trembling. In his features — as in those of the man without eyelids, incidentally — I thought I saw something familiar, but I didn't know what. The man came up to me and said in a hoarse voice: "Stranger, you mustn't stay here. Go away as quickly as you can. If you stay, he will make you drink his wine."

Surprised, I told him I had already drunk of this wine. Thereupon, the man collapsed in the dust and began to groan: "Woe betide you, woe betide you who have drunk of this wine. You will become like me." Then I recognized his voice. I recognized his face. I recognized this man. This being shaken by an incessant trembling and this other without eyelids were me. These two wrecks were me.

How do you like my wine? My wine! My wine!

The man vanished and I began to yell like a maniac. I threw myself down flat on my stomach and began to dig the earth furiously. A stream of wine spurted from the dust, but I dared not touch it. I got up and ran off. I soon came to the foot of a mountain. The two men I had met earlier were seated on a big stone. When he saw me coming, the man without eyelids approached me and said: "Whatever you do, don't try to reach the top of this mountain. Now you have drunk his wine it's too late. It's too late. It's too late. You are in the abyss and you must die there."

The voice that I had not heard for a good while made itself heard: "I told you you were as weak as a little animal. How do you like my wine? You are going to die in terrible pain and I shall have the pleasure of watching you die in the same way as the dancing mouse. Exactly like the dancing mouse. You are going to burn. You are going to burn."

I started climbing the mountain while the two men burst out sobbing. But the ground seemed to give way beneath me and I had great difficulty in walking.

"Don't try to climb that mountain. I don't want

you to. I don't want you to come back to life. You have
to die. You must die. I order you not to climb that
mountain.'' I wanted with all my strength to reach the
top of the mountain and I went forward in spite of
everything, in spite of my fatigue, in spite of the
ground that shifted under my feet. The pains suddenly grew worse and I thought I was dying. A terrible
nausea came over me and I began to vomit. The pains
gradually went away and I opened my eyes.

I was stretched out on the living-room floor and
Gerblicht was bending over me. When he saw that I
was throwing up his wine, he stopped laughing and
hurriedly stood up. Worn out, I stretched out my hand
for him to help me up, but he jumped on me like an
enraged beast and began to strike me. ''Dog,'' he
cried, ''you aren't dead. You have thrown up my wine
and you're not dead.''

He struck me so hard that I lost consciousness.
When I was found in the evening I was stretched out
in a lake of filth, yelling that I didn't want my eyelids
to be torn off.

I never saw Gerblicht again. Nor did I ever look for
him. I concluded that he had fled to another country
and I tried to forget him.

But yesterday a terrible thing happened. While I
was away my wife, whom I adored, received a bottle
of wine from Germany . . . .

SIXTH DRINKER:
THE GHOST OF DON CARLOS

My Uncle Ivan was famous. Everyone knew him, but no one ever talked about him in public. My Uncle Ivan was a spiritualist. People said he was able to communicate with the souls of the dead, thanks to a gift that some Hindu princess had once given him. In fact, my uncle really did possess this gift. In my childhood— my uncle disappeared when I was barely fifteen—I was present at some very extraordinary séances.

Having lost my parents when I was very young, I was taken in, taught about life and cherished by my Uncle Ivan. In spite of all the horrors told about him —for example, that he was a man who respected neither law nor religion—my Uncle Ivan was an admirable man in every way.

A very learned man, he was the best teacher imaginable. He was able to explain the most complicated things in a very simple, very clear manner, which enabled me, with the intelligence and few talents God had given me, to make pretty rapid progress in every area and, above all, in the field of science.

My uncle always refused to talk to me about his gift. When I broached the subject he got angry (his angers were terrible) and told me that he would never, absolutely never disclose his secrets to me. I can still hear him shout: "You want to become a medium, like me? Poor, poor child, you don't know what awaits you. You will never become a medium. I shall always refuse to pass on my gift to you, because that's what you want, isn't it? I love you far too much. I love you far too much."

Every Friday evening—why Friday I don't know— a group of six to a dozen people would invade the parlour of our house and my uncle would invoke the spirits. I have seen truly tragic things happen during these extraordinary séances. I have seen women faint when they saw their husband, their son or their mother appear before them. I have seen otherwise very brave men get up and leave the house uttering groans of terror because someone, a dead person from the other world, had touched them. I have even seen a woman in tears passionately embrace the image of her deceased husband. But the most frightening, the most terrible and terrifying thing I ever saw in that accursed parlour was the ghost of Don Carlos.

*   *   *

One day Isabella del Mancio, one of the richest and, it was said, one of the most beautiful women in Spain, came to visit out little country. Polished gentleman that he was, our Prime Minister had prepared a splendid dinner in honour of this noble lady. Unfortunately for him, my Uncle Ivan was invited to the banquet. My Uncle Ivan, despite the fact that he was, as I have said, an admirable man, was not at all sociable. He really wasn't made to live in society. His reputation for being unsociable was well founded. My uncle preferred the company of his books and, I can say so without false modesty, my company to that of those "intolerable aristocrats", as he used to call them. Therefore he was not at all pleased to receive the Prime Minister's invitation. "You ought to feel flattered," I told him, "that a prime minister invites you to dine in the company of the most beautiful woman in Spain." My Uncle Ivan smiled and said gently: "The most beautiful woman in Spain, my boy, is not Isabella del Mancio. The most beautiful woman in Spain . . . " My uncle closed his eyes and said in a low voice: "I will show her to you one day."

My Uncle Ivan declined the invitation, pleading a severe migraine.

But Isabella del Mancio was crazy about spiritualism. She had heard of my Uncle Ivan and was absolutely determined to make his acquaintance. When she saw that my uncle was not present at the banquet given in her honour she was very annoyed.

Immediately after dinner she demanded that the "sick man" should be sent for. "I have travelled thousands of miles to meet this medium" (here the Prime Minister was somewhat offended); "I finally get to this miserable country and I'm told this gentleman doesn't want to see me on the pretext that he has a severe migraine. Don't people know how to live in this country?"

My Uncle Ivan refused categorically to come to the Prime Minister's house. However, he agreed to invite Isabella del Mancio to the spiritualist séance the following Friday. That evening, before going to bed, my Uncle Ivan made a strange remark. "I hope," he said, "this Isabella del Mancio doesn't know about the ghost of Don Carlos."

*   *   *

The first thing Isabella del Mancio talked about the following Friday was the ghost of Don Carlos.

*   *   *

My uncle paled and his cheek muscles quivered, in him always a sign of intense nervousness. Isabella del Mancio noticed it. This ghost must be very terrible to make my Uncle Ivan turn pale! But I shall try to report as faithfully as possible the conversation which then took place between Isabella del Mancio and my uncle.

"I see," she said, "that Don Carlos' reputation is well established. All the mediums seem to know him and all of them refuse to have dealings with him. But I dare hope that you, who are perhaps the most . . . "

"I beg you, madam," cut in my uncle, "not to ask me . . . "

"But Don Carlos can't be so terrible."

"Yes, madam, he is."

"How can you know? Have you seen him?"

"I have seen him. And even if I had not seen him I should still refuse to contact him. The name of Don Carlos is tabu in the domain of spiritualism. One can only make him appear once and . . . As you said just now, all the mediums know him, but none will have anything to do with him."

"Then how is it that you have seen him?"

"That would be too long a story to tell. Besides, I prefer to forget it. Or at least, I should like to try. Because you cannot forget Don Carlos when you have seen him, even if it was only once in your life."

"Tell me what he is like, at least."

"I beg you, madam, if you continue to ask questions I shall get annoyed."

Isabella let the matter drop. The séance began and was not a great success. Isabella del Mancio had taken part in an incredible number of séances of this sort and nothing could interest her any more, nothing except the ghost of Don Carlos. My Uncle Ivan could see this clearly and seemed to be prey to great anxiety during the whole evening. The séance ended with the appearance of the soul of Isabella's father. But Isabella didn't even speak to her father; she had seen him so many times since his death that she had nothing more to say to him.

Before the guests left, I saw my uncle go up to the Spanish woman and ask her something. Large beads of sweat were running down his forehead and his voice was weak.

Isabella smiled and came and sat next to me, on a big divan close to the fireplace. "Your uncle seems very much on edge," she said to me teasingly. I felt that something horrible was going to happen because of this woman. That was when I began to hate her.

When everyone had left, my Uncle Ivan joined us on the divan. He took the hands of the beautiful Spanish woman between his own. "I can show the ghost of Don Carlos, if you wish," he said. "I am old now and spiritualism is beginning to bore me. You see, Don Carlos' ghost is the last thing a medium can call up. When he receives his gift, the medium undertakes to communicate with this ghost once in his life, and he is obliged to keep his promise. Afterwards, everything is finished for him."

I thought at that moment that a medium lost his gift when he called up Don Carlos' ghost . . . Oh, if I had only known! If I had only known!

"My career is drawing to a close," continued my uncle, "and I have decided this evening to crown it by calling up the ghost of Don Carlos. I have insisted on doing it in secret, because you cannot show Don Carlos' ghost to just anyone. You have to have tremendously strong nerves. If you wish to see Don Carlos, you shall see him. But I warn you: what you see will be terrifying." And Isabella burst out laughing. "Nothing can frighten me," she said. "Not even the devil in person!"

I tried to dissuade my uncle from carrying out his plan, but in vain. It was no use my telling him it would be a pity to lose his gift on account of a rather too beautiful Spanish woman who wouldn't even thank him. Nothing had any effect. "The time has come for me to call up Don Carlos," he replied.

Isabella del Mancio seemed very happy at the prospect of being able at last to contemplate the famous ghost of Don Carlos. What did the price of this apparition matter to her? "I've been hearing about him for so long." And a smile flitted across her sensual lips. "They say he's very handsome."

"No," cried my Uncle Ivan, "Don Carlos is not handsome!"

*   *   *

My Uncle Ivan told me to put out all the lights in the house and close all the doors and windows. We lived in an enormous house by the sea, a big isolated house that might have been three or four hundred years old. "When you come back to the parlour," he said, "shut the door behind you, put out all the lights except the one above the round table, and hide in the darkest corner of the room. Whatever you do, don't show yourself. Under no circumstances, understand? Under no circumstances!!"

When I came back to the parlour, my Uncle Ivan was standing in the middle of the room looking at the huge mirror hanging above the fireplace. "That's the way Don Carlos will come," he said at last.

Isabella started to laugh (all that woman could do was laugh!) and declared that she absolutely must buy the mirror when it was all over. "I want to take Don Carlos away with me," she declared. My uncle looked at her severely. "When you have seen Don Carlos," he said, "you certainly won't want to take him away with you."

I hid behind a curtain, in a very dark corner of the room, while my Uncle Ivan and Isabella sat down at the round table. "Before we begin," whispered my uncle, "I must warn you of one thing. Don Carlos must not know that we are here. Don Carlos must not see us. When you see him, don't make a sound. Above all, don't speak."

"What a pity," exclaimed Isabella throwing back her head. "When I wanted to seduce your ghost."

How I hated that woman. How I hated her.

My uncle spread out his hands on the round table and told the Spanish woman to join her fingers to his. Then he uttered some words that I didn't understand and that Isabella seemed to find very funny. I saw her laughing as she watched my uncle recite his incantations. If I had been able at that moment to foresee what was going to happen, I should have killed Isabella del Mancio and I should have saved my Uncle Ivan.

*   *   *

To begin with, all I heard was a slight, almost imperceptible sound that seemed to come from above the fireplace. My Uncle Ivan leaned towards Isabella and whispered: "Don't look at the mirror immediately. I shall tell you when you can look." Isabella turned away her head, but I continued to look in the direction of the mirror. The same low sound was repeated several times over and a soft orange light suddenly lit up the mirror. My uncle continued to mumble incoherent words. He did not look in the direction of the mirror either. But I looked.

Suddenly my Uncle Ivan jumped up and threw himself on me like a madman. "Don't look at the mirror," he cried. "Don't look at the mirror. He might kill you. Don Carlos might kill you."

At the same instant, a terrifying noise filled the

room and the mirror was smashed in pieces. A violent gust of wind lifted the curtains while a piercing whistle rent my ears. "Disaster," cried my Uncle Ivan. "The mirror is broken! Don Carlos won't be able to leave!"

A long trail of bluish smoke was hanging in the middle of the room. "He is already here," said my Uncle Ivan. "Whatever you do, don't make a sound. Under no circumstances." He went and sat down in his chair, under the lighted chandelier, beside Isabella del Mancio. Isabella seemed to be enjoying herself mightily.

The trail of smoke eddied in the room to form a long spiral starting from the ceiling and ending on the floor. The spiral swirled faster and faster. There was a sound like the whistling of a hurricane that came closer every second. At a certain moment, the trail of smoke spun round so fast that it was no longer visible. It had become a sort of transparent blue light. Then I heard the most fearsome neigh it is possible to imagine. It sounded at one and the same time like the cry of an animal and the noise of thunder.

Within the bluish light, the vague shape of a white horse was moving. It was a magnificent animal with an extremely long mane and a superb tail. "What a fine horse," whispered Isabella del Mancio.

"Keep quiet," replied my uncle. "Do you want to bring disaster upon us?"

The horse neighed again and began to trot around the parlour. It circled the room two or three times, then went and stood in the blue light again. Then it raised its head towards the ceiling and neighed quite softly.

Then there appeared the most extraordinary and the most repulsive being it has ever been given to a human being to see. It was not a man, it was a veritable Titan. Seated on the horse, Don Carlos appeared even bigger than he must be in reality. His head almost touched the ceiling. I had never seen such an ugly face or such a vicious expression. I cannot describe here the horror this giant inspired in me. He was ugly, with an almost unbearable ugliness, and his extraordinary size added still further to this ugliness. He gazed around him as though looking for something that he couldn't find. His forehead was creased and he seemed angry. He dismounted from his horse and circled the room, as the horse had done before.

Isabella del Mancio was no longer laughing. She was extremely pale and clutched my Uncle Ivan's shoulders.

Don Carlos seemed to be more and more furious. He remounted his horse. The horse walked slowly towards the mirror. But suddenly Isabella rose and approached the horse. Neither my uncle nor I could suppress a cry of amazement. We cried out just as Isabella touched the horse with the tips of her fingers. The horse reared up as if a hand of fire had touched it. Don Carlos turned towards Isabella, seemed to see her for the first time and bent down to her. He looked her straight in the eyes. Isabella seemed to be hypnotized by his look and did not move. Don Carlos took off his right glove and placed his hand on Isabella's face. His nails sank into the young woman's flesh and, as Isabella screamed with pain, five trickles of blood ran down her face.

Unable to restrain himself, my Uncle Ivan threw himself upon Isabella del Mancio. He tried with all his strength to snatch her from the ghost's clutches, but to no avail. Then he ran to the fireplace, picked up an enormous candlestick and struck Don Carlos on the left arm. Don Carlos opened his mouth, but no sound came out. Finally he let go of poor Isabella, who collapsed on the floor. A few shreds of flesh remained clinging to Don Carlos' nails. My uncle dropped the candlestick, shouting: "Run! Run, before it's too late! Don Carlos has seen us! We're lost! . . . No, there's one chance. Open the window wide. Don Carlos will think it's the mirror and jump through it."

Meanwhile, Don Carlos, who had dismounted

from his horse, had gone to the mirror and observed that it was broken. He turned slowly and looked at my uncle, still holding his left arm. "Quick, hurry," cried my uncle.

I rushed to the nearest window and threw it open. The wind blew into the room and frightened Don Carlos' horse. The animal seemed incredibly frightened. It began running about the room in all directions, knocking everything over as it passed. Don Carlos seized it by the mane and climbed onto it. My uncle had squeezed up against the wall to avoid the horse. "Run! Run! Don Carlos is angry! Nothing can stop him now! The mirror is broken! Don Carlos cannot leave!"

Then I watched the most horrible sight of my life. An atrocious vision that has left in me an infinite vertigo of sorrow and horror. Don Carlos' horse galloped about the room in all directions while his master kept turning round in order not to lose sight of my Uncle Ivan. My uncle ran to avoid being trampled on by the maddened beast. The crushed and bleeding body of Isabella del Mancio lay by the fireplace. I was hidden behind my curtain and could not move, paralysed by all the horrors I was seeing.

At a certain moment, the horse passed very close to my Uncle Ivan. Don Carlos bent down, picked him up and laid him across his saddle, in front of the pommel. I let out a great yell and hurled myself at the animal. But it was too late. Don Carlos had seen the window and his horse was already through it. "Goodbye," cried my uncle. "I loved you too much . . . "

Next day, in the village, a fisherman swore he had seen a horse galloping on the sea. Two men were on the horse. One seemed to be very tall. The other was not moving. He seemed to be dead.

THE DRUNKARD

A drunkard entered the tavern and all the drinkers fell silent. Everyone watched him sit down at the centre table, the table that was always unoccupied—no one knew why—that all the customers avoided and that everyone would have liked to see disappear. And the drunkard ordered a drink. He drank the pale ale, so light and so fresh, that had given the tavern its reputation. The ale that was said to be magic because it lulled you languorously and caused you to see visions. No one spoke any more after the arrival of the drunkard. The drunkard didn't look at anyone. He looked at his glass. Every now and then he took a sip of ale. You could feel that everyone was in a hurry to see his glass empty and to see him leave, the drunkard who was preventing them from talking.

Big Marie would have liked to go on telling her Jules what she really thought of him—now that she had made up her mind to—but she couldn't. She had stopped foolishly at the beginning of a sentence and she couldn't go on. She watched the drunkard's glass. She would have liked to be able to stand up, go over to the table, knock over the glass, yes, knock it onto the floor, spill the ale everywhere and then put the drunkard out of the door. But she couldn't do that either. Marie was exasperated at feeling so helpless.

When closing time came, the tavern keeper was unable to tell his customers that he had to shut the tavern and no one left. The drunkard ordered another ale, then another. The drinkers were tired; they all wanted to go to bed, but the drunkard continued to drink without taking any notice of them.

Jimmy—he was the local wag—had stopped right in the middle of the best joke he had ever thought of. A story about a doctor and a nurse, very bawdy and very funny. He was impatient; he was almost twisting about in his chair; he tried to attract the attention of the other drinkers; he—he too kept his eyes on the drunkard's glass.

Lucie—you know little Lucie, who arrived from the country one day and never left again because she had fallen in love with the tavern keeper—Lucie was very pleased at first that everyone had fallen silent. Lucie liked silence. She never spoke. Not because she never had anything to say, but simply because she never felt the need to say it. But suddenly she had had a need to say something. She didn't know what it was, but she knew quite well that it was very important. Quick! Quick! Let him finish his ale! Let me speak, let me say it at last! Let me say it at last!

The drunkard continued to drink. The glasses were piling up on the table and even around it and no one was speaking. When the drunkard finished a glass you could see a light go on in the depths of the drinkers' pupils. But when the drunkard called out: "Same again," eyes misted over, bodies bent a little more.

Little by little, dust, dirt and damp took possession of the place. Spiders set up their headquarters on a table and wove their webs everywhere. The drinkers no longer looked at the drunkard; they knew they could expect nothing more. They looked at each other. They watched each other grow old.

PART TWO
Stories Told For Drinkers

LADY BARBARA'S LAST OUTING

"I tell you I'm not responsible! None of what happened was my fault! It was They who gave me orders! I couldn't refuse. I couldn't. For hours I've been trying to make you understand that I played no part, or almost no part in the whole thing and you still refuse to believe me. How do you expect me to tell you where Lady Barbara's body is, after what I've just told you? I don't know where Lady Barbara's body is. No! No ! Lady Barbara isn't dead. I was supposed to kill her but . . . You know what happened, I've told you over a hundred times. Let me rest for a while, I'm so tired. No, no, I tell you, she isn't dead. Lady Barbara isn't dead."

*　　*　　*

The High Priest rose—it is so rare for the High

Priest to rise from his throne to give orders that I understood immediately that my mission was going to be of the highest importance—and he looked me straight in the eyes. It was the first time that the High Priest, the Supreme Head of all the Brotherhoods, had spoken to me. I could not help trembling and I lowered my eyes. "No," cried the High Priest, "raise your eyes and look at me well. We don't like cowards, you know. There is one test left for you to pass before being admitted to the Third Brotherhood of the Left. This test will be very difficult, I warn you, but if you succeed in your mission—and you must succeed, do you hear, you must—you can then become a Brother of the Third Brotherhood of the Left and wear the white robe that defies Time and Death."

The High Priest descended the few steps that separated us, came and stood in front of me and placed his two hands on my shoulders. An extraordinary force emanated from his whole being and I felt a fluid, an unknown energy penetrate me. All my nerves were taut and my brain was paralysed as though from the effect of a powerful electric current.

The High Priest had no further need to speak. In my head crazy images, vague ideas, incomprehensible messages jostled each other at a vertiginous speed. After a few minutes, however, an image detached itself from the inextricable tangle in my head and imposed itself on my brain. It was the image of an old woman, about a hundred years old, seated in a wheelchair playing cards. I recognized Lady Barbara, the most redoubtable woman in the entire territory this side of the Mountain With No Summit.

And I understood that I had to kill Lady Barbara.

*   *   *

Lady Barbara was one of the most highly thought of women in London. No one had any inkling that she led a double life, that she was a member of the First Brotherhood of the Right, the brotherhood of the Heads of the Universe. Every day she received in her drawing room the most important people from London and abroad. But no one knew that only her body presided over these receptions. When she seemed to be asleep in her armchair people said: "Lady Barbara has fallen asleep. That's understandable at her age." But Lady Barbara was not asleep at such moments. Her spirit had left her body to join the Brothers of the First Brotherhood of the Right, who had just transmitted a message to her. And the gathering continued, but a little less noisily in order not to wake this dear Lady Barbara, who persisted in giving receptions in her apartment in spite of her ninety-nine years.

Lady Barbara was one of the Supreme Heads of all the brotherhoods of the Cosmos and the most powerful woman in the Universe. But the High Priest had said that she had grown too old and too demanding. She was even suspected of wanting to make a revolution among the lower brotherhoods, in order to put herself at their head, depose the High Priest and take his place.

And that was why Lady Barbara had to disappear. And I was the one who had been chosen.

*   *   *

Had it not been for the slight quiver of the curtain that covered it, when I happened to glance in the direction of the door, I should never have suspected that I was being watched. Who was behind that curtain? I had been warned to distrust Lady Barbara's house, that it was full of trapdoors, windows creating an optical illusion, dead-end corridors,

secret chambers, false doors, false pictures, false
mirrors, in fact that everything in it was false and
dangerous. So Lady Barbara wanted to see what I
looked like before admitting me to her apartment? I
jumped up from my armchair and rushed at the curtain to surprise this envoy charged with describing
me to the woman I was to kill. I pulled the curtain
aside and stood petrified before the spectacle that
presented itself to me.

Lady Barbara herself, seated in her wheelchair,
wearing a black dress with a scarf of the same colour
knotted round her neck, with a strange bird on her
right shoulder, her hands holding a large volume on
her knees, Lady Barbara herself was looking at me
with her only sound eye, and Lady Barbara was
laughing derisively.

"You are very quick, young man," she said in a
raucous voice somewhat reminiscent of the cawing of
a crow. "And you are a little too jumpy. Is that the
way to present yourself before a woman who will
soon be a hundred? You might have made me die of
fear. Please push my wheelchair close to the sofa,
will you?"

Who had said that Lady Barbara was "A charming little old lady, a bit like a grandmother hen"?
Lady Barbara was frightful to see! Her hands alone
—long hands, the longest hands I had ever seen,
with hooked fingers and nails—conjured up all sorts
of visions of horrible sabbaths, bloody sacrifices and
tortured flesh. And that dead eye, half closed, dan-
gling over her cheek . . . But was this the Lady Barbara who received every evening, the slightly crazy
little old lady who fell asleep in the middle of her
receptions? Was it possible that this frightening
body inspired sympathy in London high society?

"Don't look at me like that," said Lady Barbara
suddenly, "and let's get down to business. I know
who you are and what you want of me."

At this moment an ironic light came into Lady
Barbara's eye, but so furtive that I asked myself if I

hadn't imagined it in my state of nervous tension. Did Lady Barbara really know what I wanted with her?

"I found it very strange," continued the old woman, "that the High Priest should want to see me in the flesh."

In actual fact the High Priest, in order to facilitate my mission, had informed Lady Barbara that he wished to see her in the flesh—that is to say with her body—at the gate of the Blue Temple. In this way I should be able to leave with her on the pretext of taking her to a meeting and so preserve myself from the evil spells of her accursed house. "It's a pretty unlikely story," Lady Barbara went on, "and I suspect a trap. Don't take it into your head to try to do me some harm, young man. I wasn't born yesterday, you know, and I can look after myself. Lady Barbara may be more powerful than you imagine."

Her eye had grown larger and she had sat up in her chair as she spoke. She seemed to grow bigger, bigger. From the little old lady she had been before, she had become in a few moments a kind of furious monster suddenly aware that it was being drawn into a trap.

"Have you come here to kill me?" she finally cried. "That's it, isn't it? You've come to kill me. Confess. Go on, confess. You can see I have guessed everything."

I tried to appear calm, to maintain a tranquil expression, but I felt my strength forsaking me at an insane speed. She knew everything! But, to my great surprise, Lady Barbara's anger vanished as suddenly as it had come. In a matter of seconds Lady Barbara grew calm and a smile, hypocritical no doubt, but nevertheless a smile, took possession of her mouth and twisted it in a horrifying way. "I was joking," whispered Lady Barbara, "I was joking. I only wanted to test you. But I see you are sincere and that the High Priest really is waiting for me at the summit of the Blue Hill."

Then she asked me to push her chair towards the door of her bedroom. "I have forgotten a few little things and I must put this book back where it belongs." So I pushed her chair to the door and opened it. While Lady Barbara went into her bedroom with her wheelchair, I cast a furtive glance through the door. And I saw with amazement that Lady Barbara's bedroom was exactly like a huge birdcage.

*   *   *

I was horribly afraid as I pushed Lady Barbara's chair along the dusty road to the Blue Hill. All around me I felt an invisible world moving along parallel with our route; a world of bloody monsters and unfathomable terrors; a world that belonged to Lady Barbara. But how, how was I going to accomplish my mission? To be sure, I had escaped from Lady Barbara's house, but were not these barely invisible beings I heard laughing and walking all around me as dangerous, if not more dangerous, than the London house? Several times my courage failed me and I almost left Lady Barbara in the middle of the road and took to my heels; to run, to run towards London, towards my house, towards freedom. A cup of coffee in the morning and the movie theatre twice a week. But I wasn't born to lead the life of a bourgeois. I was born to traverse time and space, to travel back up the river of life to its source and to don the white robe of the Brotherhoods of the Cosmos. I was born to soar above my fellow men. That is why I pushed Lady Barbara's chair to the top of the Blue Hill. That is why I wanted at all costs to succeed in my mission. I had to defy Lady Barbara's world and I did so.

"Here we are," said Lady Barbara. "The temple is closed. Hasn't the High Priest got here yet?" I discerned behind this commonplace question, behind this would-be neutral voice, a note of irony, a drop of acid that made me shiver. "Let us wait," said Lady Barbara. There was no more movement around us. They too had stopped.

I heard whispering, I felt things brush against me. I decided to act quickly before I went mad. I was standing behind Lady Barbara's chair and I thought that a well-placed blow with a dagger at the base of her neck would instantaneously rid me of Lady Barbara's body. As for her spirit . . . The High Priest had taught me the formulas that paralyse spirits and those that destroy them forever.

I furtively slipped my hand inside my coat and drew my dagger. At the moment when the blade entered Lady Barbara's neck and dug in it the passageway for death, a deafening clamour filled the Blue Hill. Lady Barbara uttered an ear-splitting scream that went right through me and I doubled up, my arms pressed to my belly.

Hundreds of arms assailed me and I was thrown to the ground. I was trampled on, bitten, my flesh was torn by dozens of finger nails, my body groped all over and horrible things filled my mouth and nose. But a voice rose in the midst of the cohort, crying that my life was to be spared. Calm returned little by little and I saw that Lady Barbara was standing upright beside me, the dagger projecting from the base of her neck.

"I knew you wanted to kill me," said Lady Barbara. "But did you dare think that such a vile and stupid being as you could ever vanquish me, the most powerful woman of the First Brotherhood of the Right? It was the first time anyone had tried to assassinate me and the adventure amused me. I gave you a chance. I played the game to the end. You have failed in your mission, my lad." So saying, Lady Barbara tore the dagger from her neck and threw it far away. Then I began to recite the formulas taught me by the High Priest. "O thou, great

M'ghara, god with the six arms, and you Beelzebub the All-Powerful; O you the Whorugoth-Shala, kings of the shades . . . ''

"Stop those grotesque litanies," interrupted Lady Barbara. "Time is short. The High Priest will be here at any moment and I don't want to meet him immediately. I spared your life so that you could tell him what you have seen." As she said this, Lady Barbara waved her arms towards the sky and her legs performed strange dance steps on the road. A bizarre music coming from I knew not where accompanied her dance and soon horrible guttural voices began to repeat all her sentences, singing them to a barbaric and unfamiliar rhythm.

"Know," cried Lady Barbara.

"Know," repeated thousands of voices.

" . . . that Lady Barbara is retiring to her kingdom and that everlasting war has been declared between the Universe and Me!"

Lady Barbara began to laugh and thousands, millions of voices joined with hers. Then I saw to my stupefaction that long wings had grown under Lady Barbara's arms and that her legs were twisting in a terrifying manner, to end up as two birds' feet.

Lady Barbara's head lengthened, while a beak grew in place of her mouth. Her body became covered in feathers and, after a few moments, her voice changed into the disagreeable cawing of a crow. Nevertheless, Lady Barbara continued her frenzied dance while the voices grew more and more numerous and louder. The last thing I remember is hearing a voice—the High Priest's voice—crying: "She has escaped. Lady Barbara has escaped. All is lost. He has failed in his task. Shame. Shame on him. Look, the stars have gone out where she passed and her shadow covers the whole sky."

*   *   *

"You can do what you want with me. I haven't even the strength to defend myself. I don't want to be asked any more questions. You will know I am right when the sky fills with monstrous beings and riders in white robes who will fight until the End. Until nothing is left. Nothing but Lady Barbara in her wheelchair, a book on her knees, a malicious smile on her lips. Nothing but Lady Barbara, who will take you in the hollow of her hand and crush you."

ANGUS
OR THE VAMPIRE MOON

I shall always remember Angus.

I shall always remember his smile and his hands that used to dance about at the end of his gestures.

And his eyes.

He showed his eyes only to me. It was only to me that Angus showed his eyes. When Angus looked at others it was not his eyes that looked; it was the eyes of the Other. I alone ever saw Angus's true eyes. Because I alone knew.

*   *   *

He often used to come to me afterwards, when it was all over.

He was always very happy at those moments. He used to smile and we avoided talking about that. But sometimes a little blood would trickle from the

the corner of his lips and I shuddered.

*   *   *

That evening I wasn't expecting Angus. And yet it was full moon. He had told me that this time he would abstain. "I want to prove to you that I can resist her," he told me. "Tomorrow evening the moon will be full and she will come for me. But I shall resist her. You'll see. I shan't come tomorrow evening. I shall stay at home. I shall say no to her."

He arrived out of breath, his eyes wild, eyes that I did not know, and he was trembling so much I felt sorry for him.

"I've come to seek refuge with you," he said as soon as I had opened the door. "Quick, let me in. She won't dare to enter your house. She knows that you know her secret. My secret."

He remained standing in the middle of the living-room and I saw his wolf teeth for the first time.

Two long fangs projected from his mouth, which he could only half close. "I swore you would never see me in this state," he whispered. "I ask your pardon for coming. But she was about to win the game: you alone can prevent me from doing this ghastly thing! I beg you, hold me back, I'm going mad. The desire is unbearable. Hold me back! Hold me back!"

He threw himself into my arms sobbing.

I was afraid. Yes, I was afraid of Angus at that moment. To feel his fangs so close, so close to the veins of my neck, filled me with terror. Angus understood, because he suddenly pushed me away crying: "Stand back. No, not you! Not you! I mustn't come too close to you. There must not be a disaster."

"She won't come here," I said.

"You don't know her," he replied.

"You told me yourself, just now . . . "

"She may find a way. No, I don't think so. She won't come. Not here."

"Sit down. Rest a bit."

"No. I must stay on guard."

*   *   *

Midnight.

She was there, at the window, and she was looking at Angus.

Angus was weeping.

"Even your friendship is powerless against her," he said suddenly. "I'm lost."

He took a few steps towards the window.

"Stop!" I cried. "I can still save you. So long as she is outside the house, she can do you no harm."

"Her eyes, look at her eyes. They are ordering me to leave your house. They are drawing me outside. I can't resist any longer. I must go out."

He had already reached the window and was already stretching out his arm to open it.

I flung myself upon him and took him in my arms.

"Rest your head on my shoulder," I cried. "She won't be able to drag you out of my arms."

"But your neck. Your neck," sobbed Angus.

"If you really have to do that tonight, it's me you will take," I answered trembling.

I heard her laughing outside. How she laughed! She knew very well she would beat us in the end.

We fought all night.

I held Angus very tightly to my chest and spoke softly into his ear.

Angus had turned his head to the wall so as not to see my neck. He was breathing very heavily and seemed to be suffering dreadfully. "Let me go," he said from time to time. "We can't be stronger than

her. I am what I am and I must do what she tells me
to do. At the next full moon, perhaps, I will try again
. . . At the next full moon.'' I told him to keep silent.
That it must be tonight or never.

And we resisted until the early hours of the
morning.

When the night began to die, Angus finally looked at me, but his emotion prevented him from
speaking and he did not thank me.

But I loosened my grip too soon. She had not
gone yet. We had thought the sun was rising, but it
was only another of her tricks. She was still there.

And as soon as I opened my eyes, a spider entered the house.

It was as big as a fist and its furry legs were
immensely long. It walked slowly, hesitantly,
stretching out its legs around it, coming silently
forward.

I saw it at once.

''Don't turn round,'' I shouted to Angus.

It was too late.

Angus had seen the spider too. He seemed hypnotized by it and didn't move. The spider came
towards him.

The spider must not reach Angus. I had to act.
To kill it. Yes, to kill it.

I took off one of my shoes and crept towards the
creature.

Angus didn't move. Great beads of sweat were
running down his forehead. He wore an expression
of horror.

I quickly raised my arm and struck the spider a
violent blow with the heel. It was crushed into the
carpet with a dry sound. A thick yellow liquid spurted from its body and stained my hand. It remained
motionless for a few seconds. I thought it was dead.
I was about to strike it a second blow with the heel
when it began to move again.

It dragged itself towards Angus, its body
crushed, its legs broken. It dragged itself across the

carpet, leaving behind it a revolting trail of yellow and red.

I hurled myself upon it and began to hit it savagely. But it kept on. Always towards Angus, who was looking at it.

"Run, Angus," I shouted. "Run. That creature mustn't reach you." And I kept on hitting the spider, which nevertheless continued to move forward.

By the time it reached Angus it was nothing but a bundle of viscous, stinking matter in which neither the body nor the legs could be distinguished.

I stopped hitting it and watched it crawl up Angus' leg. Angus was no longer looking at it. It was me he was watching. And his eyes no longer had any expression.

MAOUNA

There. It's done. I'm dead. In reverse. I'm dead in reverse. The ashes of my body have fled to the four winds and there is nothing left of me, but me.

You don't know it yet, you who killed me, but I am still standing on the pyre and I am looking at you with my long hands. Oh, how I hated you, and how I still hate you. You don't know it yet, you who killed her, but Maouna is more alive than ever. The flames of your pyre have not killed Maouna. Maouna is immortal. I am immortal. My body no longer exists, but I remain. More terrible and more malevolent, uglier and more dangerous than I ever was.

Go on, dance around my pyre. Laugh, sing ballads about Maouna the sorceress, who ate little children and made priests damn themselves. Do you imagine it is enough to burn Maouna for Maouna to disappear forever?

The moon is my sister and the tides will listen to me.

Maouna is no longer the one whom people strike.
Maouna is no longer the one whom people insult.
Maouna is no longer the one whom people curse.
Maouna is no longer.

You will know fear. Fear will be your bread. And you will die from it. All of you, you will die from the fear I have injected into you. I have long teeth and my poison is mortal.

Your universe will be seething with worms and grasshoppers and madmen will be the most rational among you; and clouds will fall from the thornbushes; and women will suckle leeches; and the churches will be full of vermin; and roads will no longer cross; and wine will taste of gall; and all the animals will rule over you because I have willed it.

I am not mad; I no longer have a body.

But I am still afraid of spiders.

You have hurt me. You have hurt me in my body. You have hurt me in my soul which perhaps existed. My hair turned from grey to black and I was cold. You were never kind to Maouna. I suffer in the past; you will suffer in the future. As for the present, it does not belong to us.

It rests with me to avenge myself and you have the right to suffer my vengeance.

Don't you hear me? Does your body still serve as a barrier, or don't you want to hear me? I don't want anyone not to want something that I want! And I want you to hear me.

Look, go on, look. Don't you see me? I am here. Standing in the middle of what was my pyre. Look, my arms are filled with calamities and my eyes are empty.

But perhaps you are not ready yet? Perhaps you would prefer to wait until after this feast you are preparing so gaily? Your last feast—I will make you a present of it. But it will be a feast after my own fashion.

And immediately afterwards, we will get to work, you and I. I to punish, you to suffer. And when you hear me laugh, you will know that I am happy at last.

I shall wear a long black veil that will cover the sky, and the sky will be caught in my nets. At last I shall be free. Free. To run and to laugh. To stretch out on the mountains. And to sing. I shall be free and you will be my slaves. Maouna will be mistress of the world. Maouna will be your god.

In spite of everything, I should very much like to sleep for a while.

THE THIRTEENTH WIFE
OF BARON KLUGG

"Karla von Kleiber, do you take this man to be your wedded husband?" How tapering his fingers were! " . . . do you take Karla von Kleiber to be your wedded wife?" And how powerful his hands were! "May God bless your union . . . " But why was it taking so long? "Karla, just think. There have already been twelve Baroness Kluggs." Why shouldn't she die right away? "They all disappeared under strange circumstances." Air! Air! "Will you take this woman . . . this woman . . . " Oh, how long his fingers were. "I love him so much, Mother. He is so kind to me." Life would not leave her body. "But he may be a criminal, my daughter." Life refused to leave her body.

And then . . .

At last! At last! It was coming. Death was there.

And it was gentle, like fainting.

When it was all over, Baron Klugg put the portrait back in its place and calmly went off to bed.

*　　*　　*

The Baroness was afraid.

When he had approached her, when he had put his lips to her forehead, when he had caressed the nape of her neck with his gentle hands, the Baroness had seen nothing.

But when he had turned around to look at her before leaving his wife's bedroom, the Baroness had seen. Yes, she had seen that ferocious look, that inhuman look that wished to disfigure her. The Baroness had felt that her husband wished to rend her face with his eyes.

She had bolted her bedroom door and had left a nightlight burning when she went to bed. In the middle of the night, at the hour when the big owl in the garden went hunting, the Baroness had heard a sound in the corridor.

She was certain that she was not dreaming. And she was afraid.

Nevertheless, now, in the middle of this ball, her husband was beside her and he was joking as he held her arm. Her husband who, the night before . . .

The Baroness was afraid.

There was a sound of muffled footsteps. Of footsteps someone was muffling. Who was walking about in the corridor like that in the middle of the night? A bird outside had uttered a cry of distress and the big owl had flown past the window laughing. The Baroness had risen and gone to the door.

But who could she ask help from at this ball? All these people were afraid of Baron Klugg. That was well known. No one would dare . . .

The footsteps had stopped outside the door of her bedroom. For a long time she had listened, with her ear glued to the door. But nothing moved any more. And yet there was the sound of breathing. He was there.

Baron Klugg turned to his wife. "What's the matter, Karla. You seem thoughtful."

"Nothing, my friend, nothing—a migraine."

"Would you rather go home straight away?"

"No, no! I'd rather stay here."

Baron Klugg raised his eyebrows. She had spoken these words in such a strange tone. Could she suspect . . . .

Suddenly, just beside her head, the doorknob had started to turn. Slowly. The Baroness had watched the doorknob turning, and the time it had taken to make a half turn had seemed to her so long, so long.

The Baroness was afraid.

The Baroness was trembling.

"Are you cold, Karla?"

"Yes, a little."

He helped her to put her shawl round her shoulders and slipped his arm round her waist. But was his caress not a little too abrupt? Was he not squeezing her waist a little too tight?

"You're hurting me."

The Count and Countess Mirmf laughed.

She had been sure she heard him swear when he realized that the door was bolted. Baron Klugg had sworn when he realized that his wife's bedroom door was bolted.

The nightingale had uttered its last cry of distress and the owl had stopped laughing. He was gravely devouring his prey, scrutinizing the night with his huge eyes.

Baron Klugg had gone away. The Baroness had wept. Not that she was sad; but she was beginning to believe that what people said about her husband was right.

She would so much have liked to ask help from someone. But from whom? Feigning a slight attack of giddiness, she asked the Baron and the Count to excuse her, and she took the Countess Mirmf with her.

"It's true," the latter said when they were away from the others. "It's true that you don't look well. Is something the matter?"

"Do you know anyone in the police?" asked Baroness Klugg suddenly.

"What? The police? My dear, we don't have anything to do with those people."

And she went off and told everyone that Baroness Klugg wanted to meet people in the police.

But instead of laughing, people looked at the Baron and Baroness in an odd way. "There's another one," they said, "another one who will disappear in strange circumstances. But she is the first who dared to utter the word police. She will pay for her audacity, poor thing."

The Baron and Baroness Klugg left the ball a few minutes later, the Baron having found his wife very much changed, very pale, suddenly.

She did not want to go back to the castle. She did not want to be alone with her husband. She did not want to go back to the castle. She didn't know what awaited her, but something told her not to return to the castle. Never again. Or else she would never leave it again. Never. Never again.

"You are thoughtful, Karla."

The Baroness had cried out.

"And far too much on edge."

The coach was definitely going too fast.

"I can't ask the coachman to go slower, Karla, I'm in a great hurry. I have something to show you."

They came to the castle.

How loathsome this castle was in the dark! The Baroness had never liked these homecomings from balls: she didn't like to see her husband's castle in the night. All those square towers, all those closed, dark windows, all those doors shut and abandoned for years made her shudder. How sinister was the castle that sheltered Baron and Baroness Klugg. And the Baroness Klugg was her. Karla. Karla was her name. Karla von Kleiber, the Baroness Klugg.

Her head was spinning.

"The Baroness Klugg disappeared mysteriously last night. Karla von Kleiber, the thirteenth Baroness Klugg, went to join the twelve others in the tomb. An inquiry has begun."

"You're not listening to me, my dear."

The Baroness jumped and noticed that they were inside the castle.

The Baron came up to her and took her in his arms.

"You're trembling. Are you afraid?"

She said she was cold.

All around the hall, the Baron Klugg's first twelve wives were looking at her and smiling with their fixed smiles. The Baroness stepped forward to look at them all, each in her turn. They all had long fair hair, blue eyes and a long neck. They all looked like her. She had already noticed that, but it was only now that this frightened her.

She felt her husband was watching her. Perhaps with the same expression as yesterday evening.

She turned round abruptly.

The Baron was no longer there.

She stood still in the middle of the hall. Alone with the twelve pictures of dead women who were looking at her with a smile. And yet she had the clear impression that her husband, too, was watching her. She felt that her husband was spying on her, hidden behind a pillar or a curtain. She dared not move. Suddenly she remembered that the Baron had told her he had something to show her. Her heart contracted still further.

At the same moment the lights in the hall went out.

The Baroness felt something brush against her hand and she cried out.

She heard a sliding sound. As though someone were dragging something very heavy across the floor. A sliding sound. Like a body being dragged along. Perhaps it was her body. Already. Already she felt that her body was being dragged along and put down . . .

In the darkest corner of the room, where the blackness was most opaque, was thickest, the sliding sound stopped. A faint light made a hole in the darkness. Just a tiny little hole. A little hole of light in the black sea of the darkness. An insignificant little hole. A shivering, grubby little hole that moved from left to right, up and down.

Baroness Klugg, her eyes wide open, made her way slowly towards this light.

A whisper.

"Come, I have something to show you. Come, Karla, come here. Closer. Closer. Come, Karla von Kleiber, thirteenth Baroness Klugg, come here. Closer. Again. Closer."

It was dark. Baroness Klugg stretched out her arms in front of her to avoid knocking into the furniture. When she was quite close to the little light, her hands touched something wet, stretched out vertically in front of her. The Baroness quickly withdrew her hands and wiped them on her dress.

Then a dozen other lights joined the first and Baroness Klugg saw her husband beside her, a big candlestick in his hand, smiling at her. "Look," said the Baron, "I've painted your portrait."

Two paces in front of her stood an enormous portrait. A long white dress. One hand resting on the dress. The other on the back of a chair. A portrait in every respect like the twelve others. A fixed smile. In every respect like the twelve others. And that expression! That expression in the blue eyes that seemed to be calling for help!

The portrait was still quite fresh.

"I have painted your portrait," repeated Baron Klugg.

The Baroness's hands were smeared with paint and she wiped them on her dress.

Baron Klugg put the candlestick down on the floor.

He took Karla by the hand and drew her away from the portrait.

"Look," he said. "See how like you they are. See how like them you are."

A candlestick was burning beneath each of the

twelve pictures and at the end of the series of por-
traits the Baroness saw a hole in the wall.

"That's where I'm going to put your body,"
whispered her husband.

While fear froze the Baroness's heart, Baron
Klugg went up to the first picture in the series and
pressed one of its corners. The picture moved aside
without a sound.

Everything began to spin around Karla. She
closed her eyes and put her hands to her throat. She
opened her mouth to scream, but she could not utter
a sound. Behind the picture, nailed to the wall and
covered by a long white dress, the skeleton of the
first Baroness Klugg was laughing silently. When
she opened her eyes, the twelve pictures had been
moved to one side and twelve skeletons were looking
at her and laughing. A suffocating odour of decay
filled the room.

"You already look like them," murmured Baron
Klugg.

All the candles went out and the Baroness began
to run.

MR. BLINK

Mr. Blink was dumbfounded. What kind of a joke was this? Who had dared . . . In front of him, on the wooden wall flanking Cedar Street, someone had pasted a huge poster and from the centre of this poster Mr. Blink himself was smiling at him. Above his photograph, in huge, bright red capital letters, was printed a staggering sentence, a sentence that made Mr. Blink's heart stand still: "Vote for Mr. Blink, the candidate of the future."

Mr. Blink took off his glasses, wiped them nervously, put them back on his nose and looked at the poster again.

He was seized with fear. He began to run and plunged into the first bus that came along. "No, it's impossible," Mr. Blink said to himself. "I was dreaming. I must have been dreaming. Me, a candidate?"

For weeks people had been talking about these famous elections. They said these elections would

surely be the most important elections of the century. The country's two major parties were about to
engage in a fight to the death, that was certain.

Mr. Blink trembled. He tried to read his paper,
but he couldn't concentrate on the little black char-
acters, which seemed to be delirious flies rather than
letters.

For weeks people had been talking about these
famous elections. "Oh, I must have misread it." The
most important elections of the century. Surely the
most important elections of the century. "It was a
joke."

The most important elections . . . He cried out.
On the centre page the largest advertisement he had
ever seen in a newspaper, on the centre page, occu-
pying the whole page, there he was. There was Mr.
Blink smiling at him. "Vote for Mr. Blink, the candidate of the future." He closed his paper and threw
it out of the window.

Just in front of him, a small boy leaned over to
his mother and said: "Look Mummy, that's the man
on the poster." When she recognized Mr. Blink the
little boy's mother rose and threw herself on the
poor man, who thought he would die of fear. "Mr.
Blink," cried the lady, seizing his hands, "Mr.
Blink, our saviour!" She kissed the hands of Mr.
Blink, who seemed on the verge of a nervous break-
down. "Come, come, madam," he finally murmured, "I'm not your saviour." But the woman cried
out, as though she were insane: "Long live Mr.
Blink, our saviour! Long live Mr. Blink, the candidate of the future." Everyone in the bus repeated in
chorus: "Long live Mr. Blink."

At a drugstore near his home, Mr. Blink bought a
bottle of aspirin tablets. "Well, well," said the
druggist, "so you're going in for politics now?" In
his buttonhole he wore a blue ribbon bearing in red
the words . . . .

His caretaker stopped him. "Mr. Blink," she
said, "could you by any chance give me a ticket for

your big meeting this evening?'' Mr. Blink nearly tumbled down the few steps he had just come up. A meeting? What meeting? No one had ever said anything to him about a meeting! ''What a secretive fellow you are. Still waters run deep. I should have guessed that important things were going on inside that head of yours. You've certainly given my husband and me a big surprise.''

That evening Mr. Blink did not dine. Even if he had wanted to, he wouldn't have had a chance. The telephone rang incessantly. Admirers wanting to know at what time he would be arriving at the big meeting. Mr. Blink thought he was going mad. He took off the receiver, put out all the lights in his apartment, put on his pyjamas and went to bed.

The crowd was shouting for its saviour. They even threatened to break down the door if he didn't answer in ten minutes. Then the caretaker said something terrible, something that almost produced a riot. ''Perhaps Mr. Blink is ill,'' she said to a journalist. Ten seconds later Mr. Blink's door was forced and the crowd carried off its saviour in his pyjamas. People thought his costume very original. How good his publicity was! Some men even went home and put on their pyjamas. Women in nightdresses came out into the street and followed the procession singing hymns. Flabbergasted, Mr. Blink dared not move, seated as he was on the shoulders of two of the country's leading journalists.

The meeting was a triumph. Mr. Blink did not speak.

The new party, the people's party, Mr. Blink's party, burst into the country's political life like a bomb. People booed the old parties and cried that slavery was at an end, thanks to Mr. Blink. B-L-I-N-K. Blink! Blink! Blink! Hurray! No more income tax increases, Mr. Blink would fix everything. No more political squabbling, Mr. Blink would fix everything. No further rise in the cost of living . . . Blink! Blink! Blink!

Once only did Mr. Blink try to rise to his feet and

speak. But the crowd cheered him so loudly and so long that he was afraid of upsetting them and sat down again.

His followers poured champagne into him and in the end Mr. Blink himself thought he was a great hero. As a souvenir of that memorable evening, Mr. Blink took home with him an enormous streamer bearing in letters two feet high . . .

Next day, Mr. Blink was elected Prime Minister of his country.

THE SPANISH DANCER

There is no day in Spain.

She was like a long, bright, virgin flame, my Spanish dancer. She licked my whole body and left it burned, bruised to death, my Spanish dancer. She danced like fire, she danced in fire, my Spanish dancer. She stood upright in the wind and cried that she was free, my Spanish dancer.

There is no day in Spain.

And I who plucked her every night, and I who died of her every night, and I who watched her dancing in the fire, in the wind every night, I knew that she would never be mine because I was not Spanish.

There is no day in Spain.

In the sky spattered with black the moon was dying of happiness and letting its milk flow over the sleeping area. In the eyes of gypsies mingled orgies of colours. And thousands of heels hammered my brain in ecstasy.

There is no day in Spain.

Her long white arms stretched into the night and her cruel hands tore the sky into shreds. And I, I watched her dancing in the Spanish night, my Spanish dancer. And when her eyes came to rest on me, her look bit my ear and I shuddered with joy.

There is no day in Spain.

She had a way all her own of calling me "stranger" that filled me with joy and hope. But the gypsies her brothers did not like me. I saw big Manuel, her father, talking to her one night as he looked at me with his eyes of coal. And I saw her smile — oh, how white her teeth were! Oh, how white her teeth were! — and reply to her father "yes" twice.

There is no day in Spain.

She came to me, my Spanish dancer, and put her hand on my shoulder. She said: "Come with me, stranger." And I followed her. Nevertheless I knew I should not be able to keep her, I knew that she would never be mine, because I was not Spanish.

There is no day in Spain.

I saw big Manuel spit in the fire, yes, I saw him spit in the fire and yet I went with her into the house. And I heard the gypsies, her brothers, singing as they wept. And I heard the guitars moaning waves of anguish. And I heard my heart telling me I was about to die. Nevertheless I lay down in her bed. And I saw the dagger gleaming in her hand. And I saw again her white teeth. But they were not white. They were red, red, red, her teeth were red! And I saw the blade plunge into me. And I saw her mouth that was bleeding at the same time as mine. And I saw pain pounce on my body like a frenzied bitch.

There is no day in Spain.

My body lies somewhere in Spain, in the Spanish night. And my soul . . . .

AMENACHEM

I shall go to the Island of Birds. I shall go to the Island of Birds and I shall say to Amenachem, the green sorceress: "Follow me, you who know the secrets of black magic; you Amenachem the Ugly, who surprise the gods and the demons in their palaces and slip into their dwellings in the shape of a seagull or a toad; come, follow me to the mainland, I need your aid. I will give you everything you want: the fabulous treasures, the incalculable riches that I hide in my cellars; my most sumptuous castles and my vast lands; and my soul. Do you want my soul, vile sorceress? I give it to you. Take my soul, take it; it is yours if you agree to cure my daughter."

If she refuses, the bitch, I shall tear out her tongue and her fingernails. I shall put out her eyes. I shall break her limbs and twist her neck.

But if she accepts, the holy woman, I shall make her the richest, the most fawned upon woman on earth. I shall drown her under a sea of sparkling jewels, of soft silks and heady perfumes.

And yet I know that it is forbidden to go to the Island of Birds and that very few of those who went there returned safely. But it is a matter of my daughter's happiness! I am ready to lose my spirit, I am ready to sell my soul that my daughter may be cured of this horrible sickness that makes her too beautiful. My daughter cannot be happy with another man than me! Her happiness is with me and it is I whom she will love! This love that she claims to feel for that prince of misfortune, who came to visit me last year and stole my daughter's love from me with a single look, must be torn out of her heart. My daughter will forget that man, I wish her to.

Only Amenachem, the accursed magician, can cure my child and bring her into my bed. I shall go to the Island of Birds, even if it costs me my salvation.

*   *   *

It was quite a little island. I was disappointed. I expected something terrible, something macabre. It was quite a simple island, almost charming. A few trees here and there and a lot of greenery. And flowers. I wondered why it had been christened "the Island of Birds": there were really no more birds there than anywhere else. I heard some twittering, to be sure, but was that suffficient reason to christen this place with such a name? Nevertheless, I had the impression that there was something false about this almost gay landscape.

The trees, the flowers and even the stones, which, be it said in passing, were of a pink verging on beige, a frightful colour that turned your stomach, everything had a spurious look. It created the impression of a delirious imitation of nature. If I had only known! Oh, if I had only known!

I found the sorceress's hut quite easily. Standing on the highest point of the island, on a bare hill, Amenachem's dwelling overhung the beach and had its eyes wide open on the sea. I knocked vigorously at the door. Amenachem herself opened it. The ugliness of this woman is legendary; even though I had never seen her except in my mother's eyes when she told me stories fit to make me die of fear, I thought I knew more or less what awaited me. But Amenachem is infinitely uglier, infinitely more twisted and dirty than she has ever been described. "Who are you, stranger?" she cried as soon as she had opened the door. "Don't you know that this island is under a curse and that no one may set foot here?" I did not answer. I couldn't. The creature who stood before me was so abject that for a moment I wondered if it were a human being. "Don't look at me like that," hissed Amenachem. "Yes, I know, I'm ugly. But know that if I wished . . . And then beauty adds nothing to my power. I prefer to be ugly so that people keep away from me. And who knows, perhaps I am beautiful when I am alone, when I shut myself up in my house with my secrets. Perhaps I am also beautiful to seduce those whom I want to seduce." Amenachem had come out of the house and was standing in front of me in the road. "You must be a very unhappy man, to come and visit Amenachem in her island," she said after a silence. "It is months, perhaps years, since anyone came to see me. I saw a ship three weeks ago, look, just there, at the tip of my finger, you see? A ship that had gone off course, no doubt. I sank it. Entertainment is so rare here. You must forgive me for talking so much, but I very seldom have a chance to chat with a human and by nature I'm . . . talkative. Would you like to come into my house? It's the best place to confess oneself, believe me. Come in."

I followed her. As I shut the door behind me I felt as though I were wiping out the whole world; wiping out the Island of Birds, the sea, the shore that could be seen on the horizon. Nothing existed any more except this hut and Amenachem, the sorceress who lived in it.

And it was true that I had wiped out the world behind me.

*　　*　　*

Amenachem was very ugly, but up to then she had not been terrible. She chatted and chatted, telling me about her day to day life and asking me for news of the mainland. "You know," she told me at a certain moment, "solitude weighs upon me, sometimes. Then I find myself a companion — for a while." The more friendly Amenachem was to me — and she was friendly — the more I felt that she was lying, the more I felt that her eyes were crying out that they hated me. I concluded that Amenachem wanted to gain time. Why? I couldn't say.

It was not until eight in the evening that the sorceress became terrible.

When the eight strokes had sounded from the clock that reigned over the hall, Amenachem suddenly rose and said: "Right, that's enough pleasantries. Now let's get down to business. I have no more time to lose. What do you want from me and what do you undertake to give me in return for my services?" Just at that moment there was a violent knock at one of the window panes and Amenachem cried: "Don't disturb me, I have a visitor. Come back later." Something moved on the other side of the window and I heard the cries of a bird. The sun had already set and I couldn't distinguish anything outside the window. "Go away," cried Amenachem. The bird flew off. It must have been enormous, because its wings flapped like the sails of a very big ship.

Amenachem seemed to be irritated by this interruption, and it was in a voice showing traces of impatience that she asked me again what I wanted from her. I told her my whole story; I told her how unhappy I was and how much I loved my daughter. Then I told her I was ready to give my whole fortune if she got my daughter into my bed. While I was telling my story, things were happening outside the hut. I heard cries, almost human voices, and things kept brushing up against the door and the windows. This seemed to exasperate Amenachem. At one moment she even cried out: "I told you to do your job more discreetly. I don't want to be disturbed, do you hear?"

When I had finished my story, Amenachem said: "What you are asking is not so terrible. I've been asked much worse things than that. You want to sleep with your daughter and you are prepared to give your fortune and even your soul for that? It's not very bright, but if that's what you want . . . I accept. And, naturally, I shall ask all sorts of things in return. You will understand what I mean when you get home."

Amenachem went over to the fire, took a torch and lit it. "Hold this torch while I put out the fire," she said. When the fire was out the only light in the hut was that of the torch, which made our shadows dance on the walls and ceiling. Amenachem took back the torch and went to the window. She made a few signals then turned to me.

At this moment I saw the real Amenachem. I cannot say that she had grown uglier, that would have been impossible, but she had completely changed. She no longer held anything back, but allowed all the hideousness of her sorceress's soul to appear and also all her hatred. Seeing her thus before the window, the torch in her hand and a horrible smile on her lips, frightened me, I who have never been afraid of anything. "You're afraid," she said at last. "At last you're afraid. Did you think you were going to get off so lightly? You ask Amenachem to do you a service, you give her a few jewels and that's that. You forget the whole business and live happily with your daughter. Oh no! Amenachem is more demanding. I'm not a vulgar go-between. I don't take what I'm offered, I pay myself."

The scene that followed was so strange that I don't know how to describe it. Moreover all that remain are vague memories, fragments of events that I'm not certain ever took place.

A violent blow cracked the hinges of the door, which opened wide, allowing the wind to blow into the room. The torch went out and we were plunged into darkness. Nevertheless I saw a shadow appear in the doorway and enter the hut. The door shut. Trembling,

I took refuge in a corner of the room. I sat down on the ground and remained motionless until the end of the ceremony that followed.

For about five minutes I heard nothing but whispers. At the end of this time there was a knock at the door. Amenachem opened it and two shadows crept into the hut. One of them was carrying a lantern that cast some light in the room, which somewhat reassured me. By the light of the lantern, I saw that the table had been pushed into the centre of the room and that a bird which was still living had been tightly tied down to it. It seemed resigned to its fate and was not moving.

I tried to make out the features of the three visitors, but their bodies and faces were hidden by capes. One of them was small and walked with a limp. The two others were tall and seemed to glide along.

All sorts of noises were coming from outside. It sounded as though an impatient crowd were massing outside the door, waiting for a very important event. From time to time one of the three visitors would go to the window and scrutinize the night.

Suddenly a great clamour broke out and Amenachem cried: "It is the hour! It is the hour when the great Waptuolep crosses the sky in his golden chariot drawn by hyena birds." She threw herself on her knees and her companions did the same. The clamour became deafening, while a golden light flooded in through the window. I heard a noise a thousand times louder than the noise of thunder. Amenachem and her companions blocked their ears. Another enormous explosion made the house tremble and the light became blinding. The door opened wide and I saw . . . well, for a bare quarter of a second . . . I saw great Waptuolep himself . . . well, I'm not sure . . . what I saw was both terrible and marvellous . . . it seems to me . . . but did I really see Waptuolep, the all-powerful god, the master of all the sorcerers that wander on this earth and in the other world? Did I really see him? I lost consciousness.

When I came to, the hut was once more plunged in darkness except for a small light shining on the table, beside the bird. Amenachem and her three companions were singing a hymn in a language that was unknown to me. When they had finished singing, they lit torches. Amenachem went to the table and untied the bird, which flew up and came to rest on my head. The smallest of the three visitors came over to me. He was holding a dagger in his right hand. When he was in front of me, he bent forward, took hold of the bird and cut its throat. The blood spattered my face and I cried out. Blood went into my mouth. At the same moment Amenachem shouted: "At this very instant, by the power of the great Waptuolep, may your daughter be transformed." The three visitors began to groan, to lament, and Amenachem performed a frenzied dance around the room.

Then, coming from very far away, perhaps from the depths of my soul, a hideous yell rang out: the scream of an animal having its throat cut, the howl of an enraged she-wolf. This lasted a very long time and hurt me terribly. Then . . . I don't remember very well. I recall abruptly rising to my feet, going to the door and opening it. But the scene that presented itself to me was so horrible, so improbable also, that I still wonder whether I was not deceived by my deranged mind. My God, was I even on the Island of Birds?

The island had become very large. The trees and the greenery had completely vanished. I saw nothing but a vast area of deserted rock, beaten by the waves of a tempestuous sea. And outside the house stood the most ghastly crowd imaginable. A gathering of monsters from the deeps of the seas and the skies, monsters from the world beyond, from those places where beings belonging to all the universes gather together. And all these monsters were looking at me and shouting things at me . . . Oh God, I so much wish that this was nothing but a dream. The sky was filled with huge birds that were screeching and diving down at me.

I ran for hours, I believe, pursued by the monsters and the birds. Then . . . I don't know. I woke up in my boat. The island had become charming again and birds were singing.

I am still on my ship. I am heading for my country. Perhaps there I shall know whether I have been dreaming or not.

My daughter is waiting for me.

*   *   *

Woe is me! I shall never shout loudly enough, never weep enough to allay the grief that rends and burns me.

I have lost everything. I have lost my fortune, my castles, my villages, my forests. I have lost the affection and respect of my people. And I have lost my daughter's soul. Through my fault, my adored daughter, so gentle and so sweet, has become an unrestrained demon, a loathsome succubus who pursues me everywhere and feeds on my body.

*   *   *

As soon as I disembarked in the port of Grenwald, I realized that something was wrong. The fishermen no longer greeted me and the owner of the tavern let me pay for my drinks, something that had never happened before. The women of the port crossed themselves as they passed close to me. And when I wanted to stay at the inn, I was told there was no room. They refused me lodging, me, the owner of the inn, me, the master of the country! I made a terrible scene, but two men grabbed me and threw me into the street. I almost choked with rage. However, I decided to return to the castle that same night and I hired a coach, which cost me ten times what it should have done.

When I crossed the drawbridge, I saw that there was no guard stationed at the usual place. The great courtyard was deserted. What had happened during my absence? Not a single soldier was on guard on the castle walls. Everything was in darkness. Not a trace of a fire, not a trace of a light pierced the darkness of the night. Then I realized with terror that the castle was deserted. What had happened during my absence? I stepped down from the coach trembling. I had not set foot in the hall when a scream rent the silence, a hideous scream; the same scream I had heard on the Island of Birds.

Immediately afterwards, at the top of the stairs, in a gallery leading to my daughter's apartment, I saw a whitish shadow move for the space of a second and vanish behind a curtain. "Is that you, my daughter?" I cried, but there was no answer. I ran up the stairs, hurled myself on the drapery and pulled it aside. Behind it was a horrible creature, a woman with a twisted body and fleshless hands whose demoniac smile disclosed long, pointed teeth; a very old woman, stinking of sickness, in whom I nevertheless recognized my beloved daughter. I recoiled with a cry. Then the demon hurled herself upon me yelling: "Here I am, here I am, Father. And I love you. You have desired me for so long. But take me. Go on, take me. Hold me in your arms and put your lips on my breasts. You have been dreaming of it for so many years. Don't you love me anymore?" The monster burst out laughing and moved a little way away from me. "I'm yours absolutely now," it went on. "I shall be always at your side and every night you will possess me. Aren't you happy? Aren't you happy, Father, aren't you happy?" The succubus threw herself upon me again and I had to suffer her revolting kisses for hours.

Oh, the abominable sensation of feeling oneself possessed by an infernal being! Oh, the atrocious pain that grips my whole body and bruises it to the verge of death! I am condemned to wander, a despicable and accursed creature, pursued by a demon that will torture me eternally, eternally.

Curses upon you, Amenachem, who have taken away from me everything I possessed and made of me the most unhappy and the most persecuted man there is.

ERIKA'S STEPS

When I arrived at the castle, Erik was away. Louis, his servant, handed me a note from him. My friend apologized for not being there when I arrived. Important business was keeping him in the town until dinner.

So I settled into one of the numerous guest rooms, the Blue Room, my favourite, and asked Louis to go to the library and fetch a book for me. But he replied that the library had been closed for two months and that the master absolutely forbade anyone to enter it.

"Even me?" I asked in surprise.

"Even you, sir. No one may ever enter the library again. Those are the master's orders."

"Does Mr. Erik still go into the library himself?"

"Oh no, sir. Mr. Erik even avoids walking past the library as much as he can."

"Do you know why the library is shut?"

"No, sir."

"All right, Louis, thank you. No, wait a minute. Is

the library door locked?"

"No, sir. You know the library door can't be locked, sir."

Left on my own, I unpacked my bags, wondering what could have impelled Erik to take such a decision, especially since the library was the finest and most comfortable room in the castle.

Then I thought of Erika. I almost dropped a pile of linen on the carpet. Could it be that Erika was back? And yet Erik had sworn to me that she would never return. I resolved to question my friend on this subject as soon as he got back.

* * *

Erik was still not back by dinner time. Around nine o'clock a messenger came to the castle with a message, a message addressed to me. I recognized Erik's handwriting immediately and guessed that my friend could not get back to the castle that night and was apologizing.

At the foot of the letter Erik had written: "You must know by now that the door of the library is shut forever. I shall explain everything tomorrow. I beg you not to take it into your head to enter that room; you would regret it. I trust you and I know you won't cheat. If you have not already realized what is going on, think of our childhood, of a certain period in our childhood, and you will understand."

* * *

All night long I thought of that terrible period in our childhood during which very strange things had happened.

* * *

Erika was Erik's twin sister. She was a spiteful, malicious child who hated Erik and me, and did everything in her power to get us punished. Erika disliked her brother because, she said, he looked too much like her. She couldn't bear anyone to be as beautiful as she was, and everyone was agreed that the twins were equally beautiful, the boy having no reason to envy his sister.

She hated me because I was her brother's friend. Erik demanded a great deal of his friends. For her part, Erika was tyrannical towards hers and she was surprised that she didn't have many. She loved to make others suffer and never missed an opportunity of pinching or hitting us and even, and this was her greatest pleasure, of pushing us down the stairs. She would hide at the top of the stairs so she could push the first person who came up or was about to go down. Rare were the days that passed without a member of the family or a servant tumbling down one of the stairs of the house.

The most dangerous stair of all was in the library. To be more exact, it was one of those library ladders that ends in a little balcony, a ladder on wheels, great fun for children but cursed by adults because it moves about too easily.

One day when I had climbed onto the little balcony to look for a book on the top shelf of the library, Erika slipped into the library and, without meaning to, she swore later, gave the ladder a violent push. I sped right across the library, yelling from up on my balcony, and was almost killed when I crashed into the big oak table that occupied one-third of the room. Erika found the incident extremely amusing, but this time Erik got angry and swore to take revenge.

Two days later, Erika was found stretched out at the foot of the library ladder with her head split open. She died during the following night, but before dying she repeated over and over again: "Erik, Erik, I hate you! I shall come back, Erik, and I shall take revenge. Beware of stairs, beware of stairs. One day . . . I shall be behind you and . . . Erik, Erik, I hate you and I shall kill you."

For some time, Erik and I were very much afraid of Erika's vengeance. But nothing happened.

The years passed. Our childhood drew to a close in the most perfect happiness. My parents had died and Erik's took me in. Erik and I grew up together and we were happy. Four years had passed since Erika's death. We were fourteen.

One day people began falling down the castle stairs again. Without understanding what was happening, everyone had more or less serious falls, with the exception of Erik and me. We realized at once what was happening. Erika was back! One evening, during a ball, Louis had fallen down the big stairs in the hall and we had heard the laughter of a little girl and these few words whispered in our ears: "It will be your turn soon, Erik."

The accidents went on for several months without Erik or me once being Erika's victim. The people in the castle even began to wonder if we were not the guilty parties.

One evening, my friend had gone into the library alone. Erik's parents and I were reading in the drawing-room when we heard a terrible noise from the library. I jumped up in one bound yelling: "Erika is there. Erik is in danger." My friend's mother boxed my ears while her husband ran to the library. But he could not open the door; it was wedged. "Erik must have pushed a piece of furniture up against the door," declared my friend's father. "This door doesn't lock. But there's no reason why . . . " Again we heard a noise in the room. It sounded as though a battle were going on and we heard Erik's voice and another one, a very little voice. "I tell you it's Erika," I shouted. "We must save Erik. She'll kill him." We could not get into the room.

The battle ceased very suddenly, after the sound of a fall. There was a long silence. My eyes were riveted to the door and I felt my heart contract more and more the longer the silence lasted. Then the door opened wide, something invisible passed between Erik's mother and me and we heard a little girl's laugh.

We found Erik stretched out at the foot of the steps, in the same posture his sister had been found in four years earlier. Fortunately, he was not dead. He had broken a leg and remained a cripple.

Erik had never told me what happened in the library that evening. Nevertheless, he swore that his sister would never come back again because she thought he was dead.

Another four years had passed without any other unfortunate incident occurring at the castle. I had left my friend's home to settle in a small property inherited from a distant uncle.

It was only a few weeks after the death of Erik's parents that I received a letter from my friend begging me to come and see him. "We are too young to live like hermits," he wrote. "Sell your property and come and live with me." I sold my property and went as quickly as possible to Erik's castle.

*   *   *

Eventually I dozed off around one in the morning. I had been asleep for about two hours, when I was woken by Louis. "Wake up, sir, wake up. Something is happening in the library."

I went down to the ground floor and stepped outside the library door. I distinctly heard voices.

"There was more noise just now," old Louis told me. "They seemed to be fighting. They were shouting, they were running . . . I tried to open the door, but it's wedged the way it was on the day of Mr. Erik's accident."

"Is Mr. Erik back?" I asked the servant while the voices continued their unpleasant murmur.

"I don't think so, sir. I didn't hear anything."

Then I told Louis he could go back to bed. I glued my ear to the library door. I couldn't catch what the voices were saying, but both of them seemed furious. Suddenly I heard a sound I knew only too well: someone was pushing the library steps. Then someone climbed the steps with great difficulty, it seemed.

I heard running in the room and the door opened. "You can go in, Hans," said a little voice. "I want you to see what is going to happen." The moment I was inside the library I let out a cry of astonishment. Erik was on the balcony at the top of the steps, with his crutches, and he seemed terribly frightened. Before I could make a single movement, the steps started to move. I rushed towards them, but it was too late. The steps crashed to the ground with a frightful clatter, bringing Erik down with them.

Erika was laughing. I heard her quite close to me but I did not see her. She was laughing in my ears, so loudly that I was dazed by it. Louis ran in, bent over Erik's body and burst into tears.

Before leaving, Erika murmured in my ear: "We shall meet again in four years, Hans."

THE WARUGOTH-SHALA

People claimed that nothing happened in the house on Rockhillborough Street and that Francis James Blackmoor was mad. He won't be hanged. He has been shut up in a mental institution for the rest of his days. People also claimed that the monster didn't exist and that Francis James Blackmoor invented it to exonerate himself. There were even those who said that Francis James Blackmoor murdered the little girl in an alley in Mill End South and that he didn't even take her to the house on Rockhillborough Street. The house was searched from top to bottom and nothing was found; the house was completely empty and no monster had taken up residence in it.

But I know that Francis James Blackmoor is not mad. I know that he did not kill the little girl and that a monster is hiding in the house on Rockhillborough Street. And I also know that I am in danger because I was present when the incident took place. And because I saw the Warugoth-Shala.

*   *   *

21 Rockhillborough Street is an old house that is said to date from the time of Elizabeth I. It is a very ugly house. No one has lived in it for twenty-five years. All the windowpanes are broken, the doors torn off and gnawed by damp. This house enjoys a very bad reputation. There is not a housewife in Mill End South who does not make the sign of the cross when she walks past it. Parents who want to frighten their small children claim that on certain nights demons from hell hold meetings in the main reception room, where they devour little children as they talk. Everyone knows these meetings take place in the main reception room, because people have often seen lights moving and monstrous shadows outlined in the windows of this room. Therefore children avoid passing 21 Rockhillborough Street, especially after seven in the evening.

I had heard that the house on Rockhillborough Street was for sale. I had no intention of buying it, but this house intrigued me. So I decided to pay it a visit. The notary had given me a key, which I had no need to use since the front door was half broken down.

It's funny how the appearance of things can change when you look at them from a point of view different from the one familiar to you. From outside, the house on Rockhillborough Street really was frightening to look at. It was a tall, wide house flanked by two flat towers, a house whose stones had grown black with time and which seemed to have difficulty in standing upright. The whole front sweated old age, decay and also fear. But when, after passing through the doorway, you entered the hall, all sensation of fear vanished as though by magic. Perhaps this was due to the fact that all the rooms were empty. I don't quite know. But once inside, you quickly realized there was nothing mysterious in this house. It was simply an abandoned house with bare walls and rotting floorboards.

And I was smiling as I began to mount the stairs leading to the second floor.

I had not gone up four steps when I heard a murmur coming from the second floor. I stood still for a few moments, trying to catch what was being said up above me, but I couldn't make out a single word.

Thinking I was disturbing the amorous outpourings of two young people of the neighbourhood, I decided to leave the house and wait until the two turtle doves had finished their little affair before returning. But a second voice coming from the same room glued me to the spot. Was it a moan? It was a faint voice, a stifled whisper mingled with unpleasant sounds of suction and the beating of wings. It was like a voice from another world. It was at once very loud and very faint, a shout and a sigh. The voice seemed breathless, on the point of extinction. This voice froze me all the more because I thought I had caught words among its horrible gurglings. German words, a whole sentence: "Wer ist's, der so mir es labt?" the voice said, which means roughly: "Who has thus given me to drink?" And I distinctly heard the reply in English: "My name is Francis James Blackmoor."

Then I heard something being dragged along the floor of the room. A door was opened and then shut. At the top of the stairs, on the left, I saw a shadow bend down and pick up the body of a child. And Francis James Blackmoor appeared, carrying a horribly mutilated little girl in his arms. How pale he was! His forehead was bathed in sweat and a nameless fear was written in his eyes. When he saw me, he dropped the body of the little girl, which rolled to my feet. I cried out. I bent over the body, but Francis James Blackmoor yelled: "Don't touch that child, she is accursed." He rushed down the stairs, grabbed the body and left the house by a door giving onto an alley.

I don't know how long I remained there, motionless, stunned by what I had just seen and above all by what I had heard. What was there on the second floor of the house on Rockhillborough Street? What terrifying thing, what abominable monster was hidden behind that door? I noticed that I was trembling and I sat down on one of the stairs. Everything was silent in the house, but from time to time I heard a rustling from the room on the second floor, a furtive sliding and also panting. There was still time to flee. I had only to stand up and go through the door. I was seized with dizziness, everything began to spin around me, the stairs gave way under my feet. When I came to, I was standing before the door of the accursed room and my hand was on the knob. I swear that it was in spite of myself that my hand pushed the door. I didn't want to know what there was behind that door. I swear that I didn't want to know.

No, no! I won't come! I shall resist unto death! No, I don't want to finish my days like Francis James Blackmoor, in a madhouse.

Oh, that voice which pursues me everywhere! Cursed be the minute when I pushed the door. Cursed be the instant when I saw it, the monster, the Warugoth-Shala, king of shades, who feeds on human blood and pursues me everywhere with the taste of murder. I know he needs me, but I shall not go. And that child he has ordered me to kill, he shall not have it. He shall not have it! Oh God, if you exist, don't leave me in this despair. Destroy the Warugoth-Shala before it is too late. For I know only too well that my strength is leaving me and that a desire to kill is gradually taking possession of me.

WOLFGANG,
ON HIS RETURN

Wolfgang has been back since this morning. I don't think those three weeks in the country have done him any good at all. He is still just as thin, still just as nervous. Still just as strange. His mother and I were counting on those holidays to give him back his health, to make him once again the little Wolfgang we still cherished not so long ago. But Wolfgang is no better. I even believe he has got worse.

He wouldn't eat. And yet he told us he hadn't had anything to eat for three days. He didn't touch the food we put before him. He said he didn't know what to do with this kind of food now. He said that his "diet" had changed and that he would be quite able to "feed" himself when the time came.

He has gone to bed. It's three in the afternoon.

*   *   *

Wolfgang wouldn't get up this morning. I only saw him for a few moments, but he looked to me radiant. He smiled at me. It is so long since my son smiled at me that I am quite filled with joy. After all, perhaps I was mistaken yesterday. I suppose he was simply tired from the long journey by train he had just made. Maybe my son is cured!

I have just been reading the morning paper. A frightful thing happened last night. Our neighbours' little boy was murdered. His body was found in the wood. It seems there was not a drop of blood left in him. Nine years old. The same age as Wolfgang.

Wolfgang is in bed. He wouldn't get up. He smiled at me and said he wouldn't get up till evening.

*   *   *

Wolfgang didn't eat. And yet he seemed very well. His eyes were shining and I saw him smile several times. He told us about his trip. He talked a great deal. He was very animated and gesticulated a lot. I have never seen him so gay. But he didn't eat. He said he wasn't hungry. Not yet. And yet he hasn't eaten for four days. And yesterday he was hungry. When I asked him what his present diet consisted of, his smile disappeared. He looked me straight in the eyes and something horrible, an impression of heaviness and terror passed from him to me. It only lasted a second, but it was enough to fill me with fright. I don't know why I was frightened. Perhaps it was because those eyes were not a child's eyes. Wolfgang looked at me with eyes that were not his. He rose from the table almost immediately and asked to be excused. He said he was going to his room. He asked not to be woken next morning. He said he preferred to live at night now.

I don't know what to do.

*   *   *

Wolfgang came to me in my bedroom last night. I wasn't asleep. He came in through the French window and cuddled up against me. He whispered things in my ear. But a strange smell came from his mouth. When he was talking, I had to turn my head away in order not to breathe his fetid breath. He told me that he had fed and that he was no longer hungry. He told me he wasn't sleepy and that he wanted to stay beside me because I was warm. But when he talked to me he didn't call me Daddy. He called me Hans.

*   *   *

Wolfgang slept all day. When he woke, a little after sunset, he was in a bad mood. He didn't come down to dinner. He said he wasn't hungry. That he would eat in a few days' time.

I think Wolfgang read my thoughts. When I went up to see him after dinner, he forbade me to send for the family doctor. He said he was very well and didn't need a doctor. He told me to sleep in peace.

The evening paper talks about the little sister of the boy who was murdered yesterday. She has disappeared since last night and a search has been organized.

I daren't even think about it.

*   *   *

And yet Wolfgang swears it isn't true. Who am I to believe? God, who am I to believe? The servant girl is absolutely sure she saw a man in Wolfgang's bed last night. She went into my son's room to make sure everything was all right. She claims that a man wearing a dark coat was in Wolfgang's bed and that he was whispering into my son's ear things that seemed to make the child smile. But Wolfgang says it isn't true. That the servant girl was dreaming. And that we ought to give her notice on the spot. No man came last night. He was all alone in his bed and the servant was lying.

I feel I'm going mad. I must get to the bottom of things. I shall spend tonight in my son's room.

*   *   *

Wolfgang is no longer. I have killed him. The servant was right and my suspicions proved correct. Wolfgang was a monster. I ought not to regret what I have done. But Wolfgang was my son and I loved him. Who will ever be able to explain what happened? Who will ever be able to tell me exactly what my son was?

Oh, dreadful night!

I hid in my son's room as I had planned. Wolfgang got up a little after sunset. He seemed very ill. He was even paler than usual and had difficulty in breathing. As soon as he was up, he went and sat at the window of his room. He gazed out into the park for hours. From time to time, he hid his head in his hands and said things I couldn't understand. They were things in foreign languages. Words recited to a strange, slow rhythm. The only word I could catch was Hans.

Suddenly, in the middle of one of these prayers my son was saying, the man was in the room. I don't know how he got in, all I know is that I suddenly saw him, behind Wolfgang. I almost cried out.

The man bent down and planted a kiss in Wolfgang's hair. My son got up quickly and threw himself into the man's arms, weeping. "At last, at last you're there, Hans!" he said, and he cried on the man's shoulder. It was at this moment that I saw the visitor's face. And it was the most beautiful face I have ever seen. As long as I live I shall never forget the extraordinary beauty of that face. The man's eyes were shining in the moonlight and this man's eyes were so beautiful it hurt.

When Wolfgang had stopped crying, the man lifted him in his arms and carried him to the bed. He stretched out alongside my son and talked to him.

That was the moment when I should have killed both of them. I don't know what stopped me. I simply couldn't move. Who was this man and what did he want? I don't know.

After a few minutes they rose and went towards the window. A cloud passed over the moon and the room was plunged into darkness for several seconds. When the moonlight came back, my son and his companion had vanished.

I rushed to the window and just had time to see them getting into a car that was standing outside the park. The car set off at top speed and I started calling my son.

I waited for Wolfgang all night. I knew he would come back. I didn't leave his bedroom window for a second.

He came back all alone. I saw him appear at the other end of the road, an indistinct little white shape in the light of the dawning day. He was walking very slowly, putting his bare feet down cautiously on the stones of the road. I went out of the house and I ran towards my son. I picked him up in my arms. I think I was crying. I didn't ask him where he had been. I didn't ask him what he had done. I didn't say anything. I only pressed him to my chest. But he looked at me with strange eyes. And I recognized those eyes. They were the eyes — so beautiful and yet so terrible — of the man who had come to fetch Wolfgang and take him to I know not what horrible place. And just at that moment Wolfgang smiled. That smile! The demon himself was smiling at me through my child. The demon himself was looking at me through my child. I saw the demon in the eyes and in the smile of my child and I killed him.

I put Wolfgang down on the ground; I took a big stone from the roadside and I struck with all my strength at the demon who had taken possession of my son's body.

Wolfgang died murmuring, "Hans, Hans, Hans."

GENTLE WARMTH

It was the first time Marie had been to the castle. It goes without saying that her parents didn't know she was there. Monsieur had a very bad reputation (everyone called the owner of the castle "monsieur" because he had a foreign name with many letters, far too difficult for the local people to pronounce) and everyone was a little afraid of him. . . . But who, what young girl brought up in a poverty-stricken little village, the daughter of a farmer and engaged to a farmer like her father, who, I say, could resist the temptation of knowing, if only for once in her life, the delights of a sumptuous meal, the sweet languor of an evening spent by a large fire, sparkling with health, in the company of a man — a little old it is true, but very well preserved and still quite good-looking — who whispers sweet nothings in your ear with a foreign accent? And, above all, who could resist the temptation of spending a whole night in a real bed?

Monsieur had promised Marie all this. And Marie had followed him.

*   *   *

In the carriage, Monsieur had been very correct, always addressing Marie as "Mademoiselle", and Marie had said to herself that after all Monsieur was not so terrible. . . . "If I had gone for a drive with Big Jacques or Clubfoot Pierre they wouldn't have called me 'Mademoiselle' and we should have been at the bottom of a ditch long ago! But it's not the same with Monsieur! Monsieur has style! People are so malicious! It can't be true that Monsieur has spent half his life in prison and only got out because he has a lot of money. . . . They say wicked things like that because he doesn't speak to everyone and that offends people. . . . No, at bottom, Monsieur can't be a bad man. . . "

*   *   *

Marie saw it as soon as she set foot in the drawing room. She opened her eyes wide and asked: "What's that?" Monsieur smiled and told her she would find out later.

*   *   *

Marie had drunk a bit too much. This foreign wine was so good! And she felt so well! If only her girl friends in the village could see her! . . . And Marie laughed while Monsieur was content just to look at her. From time to time, Marie thought: "He hasn't kissed me yet. He's a real gentleman." And this made her laugh all the more.

But Marie was beginning to be hungry and she asked if they were going to sit down to a meal soon. As though this was all he had been waiting for in order to act, Monsieur immediately rose and went down on his knees. Marie was a little surprised and, it must be said, very much embarrassed by this sudden

attitude. Then Monsieur began to pour out a flood of
high-flown and pretentious phrases, his hand on his
heart, his eyes turned up to heaven and all the rest of
it. . . . He promised her the world and more, and even
a pair of new clogs twice a year! All this humbug
bored Marie beyond belief. Fine manners, fine
phrases are great, but when the time comes to act,
these gentlemen. . . . In spite of herself Marie's eyes
had once again come to rest on the thing by the fireplace. . . . It was. . . . it was . . . it was . . . yes, it was a
dress, no doubt about that. But a very strange dress!

"You're looking at the dress?" Monsieur asked
suddenly, stopping in the middle of a poetic flight. "It
intrigues you, doesn't it?"

"Yes," answered Marie in a low voice.

"Come closer. You'll see how beautiful it is."

It really was a marvel. It was a dress of metal, of
copper explained Monsieur, describing it as he stood
beside the burned out fire. A dark-brown dress, inlaid
all over with precious stones, with long, ample, rigid
folds. Marie had never seen anything so beautiful.

"And it really is a dress, isn't it?" she asked when
Monsieur had finished describing it and boasting of
its charms. "A dress you can . . . wear?"

Already, Marie wanted to try it on. She was
assailed by an imperious need to feel herself in this
dress and her eyes almost begged Monsieur to invite
her to try it on. But Monsieur said nothing. If Marie
had been a little more observant she would have per-
ceived a trace of irony in Monsieur's expression as he
rested his blue eyes on her. But she was so keyed up,
she so much wanted Monsieur to invite her to . . .
Finally, unable to stand it any longer, she said:
"Could I try the dress on please, Monsieur?"

"By all means," exclaimed Monsieur with a smile
that split his face from one side to the other.

Marie observed that the buttonholes were fitted
with locks and keys and that the dress opened like a
metal box, creaking as it did so, but she didn't take
much notice of this.

When the dress was open like a trunk stood on end, Marie slipped into it, raising her arms a little to get them into the sleeves. The dress closed with a dry clack. Surprisingly, the space was very confined inside the dress, although from the outside it looked very ample. And the long sleeves were rigid, which meant that Marie had to keep her arms stretched out from her body in a rather uncomfortable position.

And it was only after it had been closed on her that Marie noticed that the dress was riveted to the floor by means of large bolts. Marie had taken off her shoes earlier in the evening and the cold of the copper plate to which the dress was bolted was unpleasant.

Marie would very much have liked to get out of the dress immediately, but she had quickly realized that she couldn't move and would have to await Monsieur's pleasure to be released. Marie was beginning to feel afraid.

Monsieur had sat down in an armchair facing the dress and was looking at Marie. He was no longer smiling. Something horrible, like hate, had glued itself to his face, which was grimacing in a horrible manner. His mouth was twisted by a nervous tic; his eyes were opened wide, almost popping out of their sockets. He was breathing very heavily and his finger nails were tearing the leather of the armchair.

Marie started to cry and begged him to set her free. . . . Monsieur quickly stood up and silenced her with a slap in the face. Then he went to the fireplace and prepared to light the fire. Marie understood what was going to happen to her and began to yell like a madwoman. The metal dress was very close to the fireplace, almost inside the fireplace. Monsieur slowly turned to Marie and said: "I'm very pleased, mademoiselle, to have you for dinner."

THE BLUEBOTTLES

The princess opened her bedroom window wide and looked at the sea.

"Already?" Ismonde the sorceress asked her. "Are you tired of him already? And yet he is so handsome."

"You know I don't like people to question my orders," the princess interrupted harshly. "Do your work and spare me your comments."

Ismonde bowed and left the princess's chambers.

"When they have all become flies," thought the princess as she gazed at the sea, "I shall change the women into spiders."

Ismonde soon returned with a small rectangular box in her left hand.

"There," she said to the princess. "It's done. One more bluebottle. It's a pity, he was so handsome."

The princess left the window, went over to the sorceress and took the little box from her.

"All right," she said to Ismonde. "You may go."
After the sorceress had gone, the princess put on a long cape and left the castle by a concealed door.

*   *   *

The cave was vast and dark. The princess, surrounded by thousands of bluebottles, stood in the centre of the cave and smiled wickedly. "Yes, my gentle lovers," she said from time to time, "I still love you and I shall always love you." She suddenly roared with laughter and opened the little box.

A tiny black butterfly escaped from the box and flew straight at the princess, who didn't even have time to cry out. The black butterfly clung to the princess's throat and killed her. Ismonde had taken revenge.

JOCELYN, MY SON

"Jocelyn, my son, was telling me just this morning . . . "

Everyone fell silent.

All eyes were turned upon Baroness Kranftung, who blushed slightly.

"That's right," she said. "I forgot to tell you that my son Jocelyn is back from Paris. He got back last night, utterly exhausted, poor fellow."

Baroness Kranftung, glad to see that everyone was interested in her son Jocelyn (when she spoke of him, everyone fell silent and listened to her), began to walk slowly around the big salon, speaking now to one now to the other, distributing smiles here and there.

"As I was saying just now, Jocelyn, my son, was advising me this morning to go and rest for a while in the country. Poor child! He knows I absolutely cannot leave the capital during the season and that I'm not the sort of woman who can rest. I think he worries a bit too much about his old mother's health."

She burst out laughing and the gems of her neck-lace tinkled. She sat down in an armchair by the fireplace, closed her eyes and rested her head against the back.

All those gathered in Princess Winterclung's salon looked without a word at this tall, gaunt woman who had been talking for years about a son who had never existed. No one dared break the silence that always followed Baroness Kranftung's monologues.

The members of Viennese high society entertained for this strange woman a feeling that lay on the borderline between affection and pity. When people spoke of her, they always said: "That poor Baroness Kranftung . . . "

Apart from her habit of claiming to have a son who was always away travelling somewhere or other, Baroness Kranftung was the most likeable and the wittiest of women. Her conversation was sparkling and she had been very popular in her youth. She was said to have been very beautiful. She had never married because, she said, men made her ill.

One day, at a ball, she had started talking about her son Jocelyn who had left the previous day for London. And since then, the Baroness had had a fresh adventure of her son's to talk about every day. She received many letters from him, she said, and her son was exceptionally handsome, well-educated, intelligent . . .

She suddenly rose and turned towards the bar. "Champagne," she cried. She took a glass and turned to the assembly.

"I have great news to announce," she said. "This evening Jocelyn, my son, is coming. He promised to call for me after the ball."

No one knew what to say. Princess Winterclung went up to her and said: "That's splendid, my dear Baroness. I shall be delighted to make his acquaintance." Then she fell silent. Two tears rolled down the Baroness's cheeks. "Jocelyn, my son, will come this evening. He promised. This evening my son Jocelyn will come and fetch me. And the two of us will go home . . . like two lovers. My son is very handsome, you know, very handsome. He is twenty-two now. He is tall; he has blue eyes and fair hair. He is very handsome. You know, Jocelyn, my son, is . . . is . . . is . . . ''

The Baroness was weeping more and more copiously. "He is coming to fetch me, you know, he is coming. He promised.''

After emptying several glasses of champagne, the Baroness returned to the armchair by the fireplace. "I'm so happy. It's the first time he has agreed . . . yes, he always refuses . . . He is a bit shy, you know, like . . . like . . . ''

Little by little people had begun talking again and the party continued, monotonous like all Princess Winterclung's parties.

And the Baroness continued talking and drinking and telling impossible stories about her son. No one was listening to her any longer and she seemed to be looking around for someone to converse with. "Jocelyn, my son . . . ''

She drank and wept the whole evening. She had never been so noisy and Princess Winterclung was beginning to lose patience. "I've never seen her in such a state. Could she be going a bit mad?''

Towards the end of the ball, Baroness Kranftung was completely drunk. She shouted, laughed, wept. She even took a young girl by the waist and started dancing . . . dancing. When she let go of the girl, the Baroness, quite giddy, began staggering and finally collapsed on the salon carpet.

She was lying on her back, her eyes wide open, murmuring very quickly: "No, no, Jocelyn won't come, Jocelyn doesn't exist. There never was a Jocelyn. He's a complete invention. I made him up because . . . because . . . No, no, Jocelyn won't come. Jocelyn, my son . . . ''

She tried to get up and her eyes turned towards the big door of the salon. She uttered a yell and fell back, lifeless, to the floor.

There, in the doorway of the salon, tall, fair, with blue eyes and a gentle smile on his lips, marvellously handsome, stood Jocelyn.

THE THIMBLE

If anyone had told Bobby Stone what would happen
that day, he would probably never have got up. And
. . . well, the catastrophe might perhaps have been
avoided.

*   *   *

Bobby Stone was a good fellow. He worked in an
office, drank moderately, went to Mass every Sunday
and had a weakness for plump women. He was
neither old nor young; he merely wore a hat to hide
his increasing baldness.

Bobby Stone didn't have the slightest idea that he
was going to be the cause of the catastrophe.

*   *   *

"Really, madam, please stop this silly game.
People are looking at us." It was true a crowd of

idlers had gathered round them and were beginning to look at Bobby Stone disapprovingly. That was because this woman was blubbering to break your heart! "Monsieur," she cried, "take it! Take it! I'm giving it to you. It's yours." But Bobby Stone didn't want it. No, not at all. "What do you expect me to do with it?" he answered. "First of all it's an . . . instrument for women." More and more people were gathering on the sidewalk and Bobby Stone was beginning to feel hot under the collar. He took out his handkerchief to wipe his brow, but did not remove his hat to mop the sweat from his head. "She's crazy. Yes, she's crazy. And all these people looking at us. I don't want her thimble!"

A man stepped out of the crowd and grabbed Bobby Stone by the collar. "Well," he said, hissing into his face, and his breath stank, "so you make women cry in the middle of the street?" Bobby Stone was trembling. "But I don't know this woman. She wants to give me a thimble and I don't want her thimble, I . . . " Really, Bobby Stone had had enough. In a sudden burst of courage—where was cowardice getting him?—he slammed his fist into the face of the man who was threatening him and took to his heels, not without knocking down a couple of people who tried to stop him.

*　　*　　*

It goes without saying that he did his work very badly that day. The columns of figures danced before his eyes, and when he closed them he saw the unknown woman offering him the thimble. "It's yours."

Five o'clock struck. Bobby Stone had collapsed in his armchair, his tie undone, one hand on his heart. "I would never have believed that such a stupid incident . . . " Oh no, that was too much, right into his office. And it wasn't a vision; his eyes were wide open now. She was sitting in the chair in front of him, on the other side of the desk. "If you don't take it right away," said the woman, "I shall be forced to forbid you to take it and then you'll run after me and steal it. I tell you, you will steal it from me." Bobby Stone jumped up, crazy with fear, and ran for the door. "Very well," cried the woman, "I forbid you to take my thimble." Bobby Stone stopped dead. Oh, the beautiful thimble. The beautiful thimble! Made of plastic with little holes in it! The beautiful thimble! He absolutely must have this thimble. Nothing else existed in the world anymore except this pink and yellow thimble. He started running after the woman, who pretended to be running away while taking care to lose ground.

Slap! And slap again! Bitch! So you wanted to keep it to yourself, eh? The thimble for you and nothing for me! Take that! And there were kicks and slaps and jabs with the knee . . .

When he left the building, his clothes were in disorder and there was a little blood on his fingernails, but he had the thimble. It was his and no one, no one, you understand, would ever get it away from him. He knew the secret of the thimble now. Before she died the woman had murmured: "In the thimble . . . in the thimble . . . I have shut up the universe."

Next morning, when he woke up, Bobby Stone remembered nothing. He found a pink and yellow thimble on his bedside table. How ugly this thimble was! He threw it in the garbage bin. But before leaving for the office, Bobby Stone pulled a button from his overcoat that had been almost off anyhow. He took a needle and thread and thought of the thimble that was at the bottom of the garbage bin. He went to look for it. And in order not to prick himself as he sewed the button back on his overcoat, Bobby Stone slipped his finger into the little thimble. He crushed the whole universe.

THE WOMAN
WITH AN UMBRELLA

"Well, that's a funny place to lose an umbrella."
He bent down and picked up the umbrella.

*   *   *

The telephone rang.
"Hallo."
"Good evening. Did you find my umbrella?"
"Pardon?"
"I asked you if you had found my umbrella. A black umbrella with . . ."
"Yes, as a matter of fact I did find an umbrella this morning. But madam, how did you know that it was I who found it?"
"But my dear sir, I lost it precisely so that you should find it. And now I should like to have it back. Will you bring it to me, please? I shall wait for you this evening in the middle of the wooden bridge, to the east of the town, at eleven o'clock. Good evening."

*   *   *

"You're late. I've been waiting for you for ten minutes."

"I'm sorry. I was held up. Here's your umbrella."

"Thank you."

She looked him straight in the eyes.

"And now, jump. Your hour has come. It's time. Go on."

He climbed over the railing and threw himself into the river.

And she walked away, leaving her umbrella in the middle of the wooden bridge to the east of the town.

IRGAK'S TOOTH

The man lay stretched out on the moss looking at this new star, almost as big as the moon; this unknown star that all the Inuit had been talking about for some time.

The whole village was asleep. The tundra was deserted. And the man was afraid. He who had never had a toothache in his whole life had been suffering terribly since the coming of that accursed star. It was a terrible shooting pain that made him almost mad with rage and prevented him from working, from talking and almost from moving.

When some cloud, come from who knows where, somewhat veiled the new star, the man's suffering was allayed and he was able to breathe more freely. But that night (it wasn't really night; at that time of year the sky darkened a little when evening came, just enough to make the moon and a few stars appear) there was no cloud and the star was shining as it had never yet shone since Irgak had first seen it. And

Irgak suffered as he looked at it. From time to time he groaned and the woman came out of the igloo to comfort her husband by running her hand over his face and smiling at him. Before going back inside the igloo, she looked at the sky and raised her fist. "Bad star," she sometimes cried.

Irgak was mad with fear. And yet Irgak was a brave man, a great hunter, a perfect Inuk who had never feared either the cold or the snow, or the wild animals. But this star that had brought him a pain in his mouth frightened him. Irgak was frightened for the first time in his life. He wouldn't sleep inside the igloo anymore. He remained stretched out on the moss of the tundra all night long, watching the star and hoping for clouds.

The whole village knew about Irgak's suffering. The shaman declared that he had never heard of anything like it and all his prayers were fruitless. The gods had not healed Irgak and the star remained hanging over the village, its round white eye fixed on the Inuk.

Then the shaman had said that Irgak was under a curse and that he would have to be killed if they wanted peace. The star wanted Irgak and he would have to be sacrificed. But the chief of the tribe had intervened and had declared that they must wait a few days before sacrificing Irgak. "If the star and Irgak's suffering have not disappeared in five days, we will kill Irgak. Not before."

The five days had passed. This was the fifth night. Irgak knew he was going to be killed. At times he closed his eyes and prayed that they would come and take him right away. But all the Inuit had retired into their igloos when the star appeared in the sky and the village was deserted. He would have to wait until tomorrow.

The woman had dozed off in the igloo and Irgak listened to her strong, healthy breathing and thought of the joys she had brought him that he would never know again. Tomorrow he would be dead and his wife banished because she was the wife of an Inuk under a curse.

Irgak's tooth seemed to want to sink right into his gum and the atrocious pain rose to his ear. Irgak did not want to cry out for fear of waking his wife. He closed his eyes for a few instants. But the pain was more acute, more searing when Irgak closed his eyes. Then Irgak had the impression that he was looking inside his body, looking for the pain in order to see it, to contemplate it, perhaps also to seize it with his two hands and pull it out. He was more conscious of his pain. He could analyse it, follow it along his gum, then into his ear and finally into his head; to say to himself, well, it has got to such and such a point and is going towards this or that other one; to feel it growing larger as it approached his brain.

Suddenly, the pain was so intense that he opened his eyes. Tears were rolling down his cheeks, big salty tears, and getting lost in his neck.

Irgak stifled a cry. The star had increased enormously in size and now was four or five times bigger than the moon. "It's coming towards me," Irgak said to himself. "It's coming for me. I don't want that. I'd rather be killed by my brothers than devoured by the star." He tried to rise on one elbow, but a pain in his head laid him low. He remained stretched on the ground, his eyes open, fire in his head.

It was then that he felt the presence of the other. He was no longer alone on the tundra, he was sure of that. He slowly turned his head towards the river and his fingernails dug into the moss. A giant Inuk was standing on the bank of the river looking at him. A very ugly Inuk with a ravaged face and enormous, thin hands. And that terrible smile! The giant Inuk had no mouth, only a small slit without lips opening upon a black hole with no teeth.

The Inuk looked at Irgak without moving. He seemed to be waiting. Irgak turned his head and saw that the star had come closer still. It was hiding half the sky, and winds unknown to Irgak seemed to be coming out of it and sweeping the tundra.

A big bird flew backwards across the sky and the giant Inuk came towards Irgak, who couldn't move, nailed to the ground as he was by fear and suffering.

The Inuk kneeled down beside Irgak and bent over him. He was so hideous to look at that Irgak shut his eyes, determined to die without reopening them. He felt a long, slender, cold hand feel his face and come to a stop on his mouth. A finger parted his lips and went into Irgak's mouth. Irgak hadn't the strength to clench his teeth. The Inuk's finger went in right down to his throat. His stomach heaving with nausea, Irgak opened his mouth wide. The Inuk took advantage of this to thrust two more fingers into his throat.

Irgak refused to open his eyes. The Inuk felt around in Irgak's mouth, looking for the tooth, Irgak's aching tooth. And when finally he found it, when his fingers touched the tooth, Irgak let out a yell that filled the tundra and awakened the wolves in the depths of their lairs. Irgak had not opened his eyes. The Inuk tugged at the tooth with all his strength and Irgak continued to yell. When the tooth was finally pulled out, the pain was so intense that Irgak lost consciousness.

The woman ran out of the igloo just in time to see a shadow fleeing towards the river. The star had vanished. A thread of blood was trickling from Irgak's mouth. A very strong wind was blowing over the tundra.

THE OCTAGONAL ROOM

As soon as he returned from his trip around the world, Frederick had invited me to dine with him in order, as he put it, to re-establish a friendship unfortunately interrupted during his trip. I had not seen Frederick for three years and I was very surprised to observe how much he had changed since his departure. This was no longer the joyful, carefree Frederick I had always known; it was a dejected, nervous, pale man; a man who had aged, too. His temples were already beginning to turn grey and wrinkles furrowed his brow and each side of his nose. This was no longer the same man at all.

The first thing Frederick said when he saw me was: "You haven't changed. You haven't changed at all in three years. Aren't you ever going to grow old?" I didn't know what to reply. I didn't want to tell him he had aged a great deal and that he looked ten years older than his real age. "I know," he said after an embarrassing silence, "I've aged a great deal. You won't recognize me, you'll see. This three-year journey, all the countries I have been to, have completely transformed me. I have a lot to tell you. After dinner I'll show you my treasures." But he didn't sound very sincere and his smile was forced.

I examined him attentively during the meal and observed that he was nervous, worried to a surprising degree. He kept looking in the direction of the dining-room door and didn't listen to half I said to him. He seemed to be waiting for someone or something. Nevertheless, he forced himself to be gay; but his expression betrayed anguish and I wondered what could be frightening him so much. Because he was afraid, I was sure of that. By the end of the meal, he was trembling and sweat was pouring down his forehead. He had unbuttoned the collar of his shirt and his hands were in constant movement, running from one glass to another, from the table-cloth to his dripping forehead.

When we left the dining-room, he was in such a state of nerves that he could scarcely keep upright.

When he had shut the library door behind us, he rushed towards me, begging me to save him, to deliver him from the frightful things that were pursuing him everywhere and ceaselessly tormenting him. I didn't understand a word he was saying and was obliged to shake him violently in order to calm him down a bit. "What's the matter with you?" I asked when he had quietened down. "Are you ill? I can't make head or tail of what you've been telling me. Explain more clearly." Frederick had sat down in an armchair and seemed to have aged by another ten years. "It's terrible," he said finally. "Sometimes I have the impression that everything that is happening to me doesn't really exist and that I'm mad. But these things are real and I can't get rid of them."

"But what things?" I asked. "What things?"

"You'll know soon," replied Frederick. "I can feel they're going to come. I didn't think they would come today; that's why I invited you to dinner. But during the meal I heard them behind the door of the octagonal room — that's the room in which they've taken refuge since my return — and I'm sure they're getting ready to throw themselves upon me as soon as my will is too weak to fight them.''

I thought Frederick had gone mad. What were these things he was talking about and why had they taken refuge in the octagonal room?

I rose and made for the door.

"Where are you going?" asked Frederick.

"To the octagonal room," I replied.

"No, no, don't go! Don't open the door of that room! Even more of them would come and they would kill me."

"But who are 'they'? What are they? You must tell me, Frederick. I must know, if you want me to help you."

"You wouldn't believe me if I told you what they were. When you've seen them you'll believe me. Don't go into the octagonal room. They will come here. You will see them. If you don't open the door of the octagonal room, they won't all come. But if you open the door, thousands of them, millions of them, will be able to escape."

Frederick had risen. He was shouting like a madman, gesticulating and almost running about the room. "You must be imagining those things," I told him as I opened the library door. "Come with me to the octagonal room. You'll see there's nothing there. That's the only way to free yourself from these hallucinations."

"No, don't go, I beg you! You'll regret it."

He followed me as I made for the octagonal room, trying to pull me back by the shoulders or by the jacket. I gave him a push and he collapsed on the carpet of the corridor sobbing. He was in a paroxysm of madness and was screaming like someone being tortured. "You'll be sorry! You will be responsible for my death! You will be my murderer! If you open that door, you will kill me!''

When I came to the octagonal room, which was at the end of the ground-floor corridor, I put an ear to the door. I didn't hear anything. Everything was silent in the room.

The octagonal room, so-called because of its eight walls and also because of the octagonal shape of all the furniture and all the objects in it, was my friend's grandparents' room. One day Frederick's grandmother, who had been a very eccentric, very strange woman, had decided to build a room which was octagonal in shape and in which would be placed an octagonal bed and octagonal furniture and accessories. She had lived very happily in this room and had committed suicide there at the age of eighty.

"I can't hear anything," I told Frederick, who had risen and was standing in the middle of the corridor, his eyes popping out of his head. "There's nothing out of the ordinary in that room."

I quickly opened the door. Frederick yelled with fear and rushed into the library, shutting the door behind him.

There was nothing suspicious in the octagonal room. But the room really was strange. I had never entered it without feeling ill at ease. I had always had the impression that this room had been the work of a deranged mind. Nevertheless, Frederick had sworn that his grandmother had never been mad. What astonished me most when I entered this room was the window. This eight-sided window looked like a ship's porthole and I was always surprised to see a garden with trees and flowers when I looked out.

I poked about everywhere, looking . . . I didn't really know what for. I found nothing. The octagonal room was completely inoffensive. I went out of the room, leaving the door open, and made for the library. I found Frederick almost unconscious in an armchair. "There's nothing in the room," I told him. "You must be imagining these things. You should see a doctor."

"Shut the door," whispered my friend. "That will

delay them a few moments.''

I shut the door and went up to Frederick. "You must tell me everything," I said gently. "I may be able to help you when I know. Tell me everything."

But Frederick refused to explain everything. He only told me these things had been following him ever since he left Africa, attacking him almost every day. "They haven't succeeded in killing me yet because they never attack in very large numbers. I've managed to kill thousands of them, but others come to replace the ones I kill, bigger ones, fiercer ones. The day they all come . . . When I got home yesterday, they settled in the octagonal room. They are sure to have multiplied during the night. They made a terrible noise in the octagonal room . . . all night long . . . a terrible noise. But they haven't come out of the octagonal room. This morning I didn't hear them anymore. Then I thought they would leave me in peace for a day or two as they sometimes do. But you opened the door for them. They will come. Oh, they will come and kill me!''

No sooner had he uttered these words than I heard an odd noise in the corridor. Frederick had heard it too. He took my hand and said: "There they are! Goodbye, my friend. This time a very large number of them will come and kill me. Do you hear them? They have come out of the octagonal room and are making for us!''

I rose and was about to look into the corridor, but Frederick looked at me so beseechingly that I hadn't the courage to oppose him.

The noise was growing louder every second until it became deafening. It was a strange noise, like that made by millions of tiny feet and tiny mouths. It was as though a countless number of tiny creatures were walking in the corridor, bumping into each other, pushing each other to get somewhere as fast as possible . . . I don't know where. There was a cracking sound as though someone were crushing tons of woodlice or other tiny insects. And this hideous clicking was growing constantly louder, coming closer and closer to the library. Frederick and I were watching the door and we were afraid. I was beginning to believe what my friend had told me.

Suddenly Frederick jumped up from his chair crying: "Look! Some of them are slipping under the door!" It was no good my looking in the direction in which my friend was pointing; I saw nothing. I only heard the horrible noise coming from the corridor. "I don't see anything," I shouted to my friend, my nerves on edge. "Yes, yes, look, they're coming towards you! Squeeze up against the wall, they'll reach you, they're quite close to you!" But I couldn't see anything! I couldn't see anything! I started yelling with fear and squeezed up against the wall.

Frederick began to run around the room. He kept slapping himself all over, as though to crush things clinging to his clothes. But there was nothing on Frederick's clothes. And that damned noise was getting louder and louder.

The library door, although it was of massive oak, suddenly began to give way under the terrific pressure of things I couldn't see. The wood cracked; the hinges were torn off. Suddenly it caved in and a wave of noise flooded the room. Frederick was no longer screaming. He seemed to be under attack by millions of creatures that were devouring him. He fell back under the pressure of these invisible creatures and began to scream again. "My mouth is full of them. My eyes are full of them. They're eating me up. You have killed me! You have killed me!"

I shut my eyes when the noise reached its peak.

THE DEVIL
AND THE MUSHROOM

He was a big devil of a devil. Like all devils, he had a
tail. A funny sort of tail. A devil's tail, a long tail that
dragged on the ground. And ended in an arrowhead.
In short, he was a big devil of a devil with a tail.

He was walking along the road and all the girls he
met ran away holding their skirts. When they got
home they cried: "I've seen the Devil! The Devil is
there, I saw him! I tell you, it's true!"

And the devil continued on his way. Looked at
them running away and smiled.

He came to an inn. "Something to drink," cried
the devil. He was given something to drink. The innkeeper was scared. "Are you afraid of the Devil?"
asked the devil. "Yes," replied the innkeeper timidly
and the devil laughed. "Your wine is good, innkeeper, I shall come back." The innkeeper lowered
his head as he wiped his hands on his inkeeper's
apron. White. But dirty. With traces of sauces, of
meats, of vegetables just pulled out of the ground,

and of coal too, because the ovens have to be lit in the morning. "This once," thought the innkeeper, "I should have preferred my wine to be less good." And the devil, who read thoughts like all devils, laughed louder still and even slapped his thighs.

But someone had entered the inn and the devil fell silent. It was a boy. A young boy with a beautiful face. "Where's that roll of drums coming from that I can hear?" asked the devil. "I don't know," replied the boy. "This roll of drums has gone with me wherever I go ever since I was born and I don't know where it comes from. It's always like that. It's always with me." The devil went up to the boy and sat down beside him on a bench. "Are you a soldier?" asked the devil. That same moment the drumming stopped. "A soldier? What's that?" asked the boy in his turn. "What," cried the devil, "you don't know what a soldier is?" The innkeeper, who had gone back to his kitchen, returned to the parlour and said: "I don't know what a soldier is either."

"Well, come on," cried the devil, "come on! A soldier is someone who makes war!"

"War," said the boy. "What's that?"

"You don't know what war is?" asked the devil.

"No, that's a word I don't know," replied the boy.

"That's quite a new word to us," added the innkeeper.

Then the devil, in a fury, holding his head in his hands, yelled: "Have I forgotten to invent war?"

In the road outside the inn a little girl was singing:
"A woman opened the door.
The Devil cried out: 'Die.'
The woman was no more.
Her soul to hell did fly."

"I want a piece of charcoal," cried the devil. The innkeeper brought him a piece. "That's not big enough. I need a big piece of charcoal. I need the biggest piece of charcoal!" Then the innkeeper gave him the biggest piece of charcoal he had. "That's not big enough yet," said the devil. The innkeeper replied: "There isn't a bigger piece. That's the biggest piece. The biggest I have."

"Very well," said the devil, annoyed, "if that's the biggest piece you have . . . "

Then the devil climbed onto the table and made this speech: "You who don't know what war is, open your ears wide." The inn parlour was full to bursting. So full the innkeeper had been forced to seat people on the ceiling. "Look at this wall," continued the devil. "With this wretched piece of charcoal I will show you what war is." Then, hurling himself at the wall, the devil started drawing furiously. The drawing he made was a drawing of a mushroom. A huge mushroom that covered the wall of the inn. When he had finished, the devil jumped back onto the table and declared: "There you are. I've drawn you a war. A small war, because my piece of charcoal is too small for me to draw you a big one, a real one." Everyone went off clapping and there was no one left but the devil, the boy and the innkeeper. "But it's a mushroom," said the boy, "an ordinary mushroom. Do you mean a soldier is someone who grows mushrooms?"

"You don't understand anything," said the devil, twirling his tail, "nothing at all. That mushroom isn't an ordinary mushroom. Do you know what a gun is?"

"Yes," replied the boy.

"Ah, at least there's one thing I didn't forget to invent. That's something. Have you a gun?"

"Yes."

"Go and fetch it right away. The war can't wait. It's late enough as it is."

The boy went off to fetch his gun, while the devil drank another bottle of wine (he was a rather drunk devil).

The innkeeper looked at the mushroom on the wall and scratched his head, thinking: "Such a big mushroom . . . how economical." And he went back to his kitchen.

The devil wasn't pleased with himself. "Idiot," he said, "idiot, blockhead, numbskull that I am. That's

why our affairs are going so badly! I forgot to invent
war! Oh, well, they won't lose anything by waiting!
I'll cook them up a real honey of a war! The real
thing! So they don't know what war is! Devil's
honour, they won't take long to learn! The loveliest
little war is going to burst in their faces. . . . ''

The boy was already back with his gun. When the
devil saw the boy's gun, his anger doubled. They
called that a gun? Did they take him for an idiot or
what? All rusty! All filthy! There were even parts
missing! The devil took hold of the gun and twisted it.
The boy opened his eyes wide and said: "Oh!"

The devil went to the fire, took the poker, blew on
it and turned it into the finest gun anyone had ever
seen. The boy said to the devil: "Can I touch it?"

"Well, of course," replied the devil. "It's yours. I
give it to you." The boy thanked him. "Don't thank
me, that always disappoints me."

The boy hugged and kissed the gun. He began to
dance, holding it in his arms as if it were a woman.
"You love the gun, eh?" said the devil. "Oh, yes,"
replied the boy, dancing. The devil stopped him with
a gesture and made him move back to the bench.
"What's the next country called? The country next
door to yours?" he asked the boy. The boy seemed
very surprised. "The next country? But there isn't
any next country. There's only one country, the
world. The world is one country. Mine." The devil
slapped the boy so hard in the face that he spun round
twice.

"Did anyone ever see such ignorant people!"
roared the devil. "The world one country? You're all
mad. Listen, in order to have a war you need at least
two countries. Let's say the village on the other side
of the river is another country. An enemy country.
And don't you tell me you don't know what the word
enemy means or I'll give you another couple of
swipes. You hate the people in the other village, you
hate them with all your heart, do you understand?"

"But my fiancée . . . "

"Your fiancée too. Her more than the others. You hate them all and you want to kill them."

The boy sprang to his feet. "With my gun?" he cried. "But that's impossible! We only use our guns to kill birds or animals. . . . "

"You want to kill them with your gun because that's how the first war has to start. You will be the first soldier."

"You mean you have to kill people to make war?" said the boy, looking at the mushroom.

"That's right. To make war means to kill people. Lots of people. You'll see what fun it is!"

"What about the mushroom?" asked the boy.

"The mushroom? That will come later. Much later. You may be dead by then."

"Killed?"

"Probably."

"In the war?"

"Yes."

"Then I don't want to be a soldier. Not to make war."

The devil climbed up onto the table and let out a terrible devil's bellow. "You'll do what I tell you to do," he then yelled at the boy.

The innkeeper came out of the kitchen. He was dragging behind him an enormous cauldron. "I want you to tell me where I can find a mushroom as big as that one on the wall," he said pointing to the mushroom. "Go back to your kitchen, you ignorant man!" yelled the devil. "It's not you that will eat that mushroom, it's the mushroom that will eat you."

The devil got down off the table, took the boy by the shoulders, made him sit down and said to him: "You're a man, so I suppose you like fighting . . . No, don't interrupt me, I understand. You never fought, right? If I wasn't damned already you would surely get me damned . . . Listen . . . You wouldn't like to see someone rise up in front of you that you had always disliked . . . There must be someone you're not particularly fond of . . . someone you could frankly hate and with whom you could fight . . . Didn't you ever feel the need to hate? The need to fight?'' The boy answered in a low voice: ''Yes, I have felt the need and I'd like to fight with . . . ''

''Who, who?'' cried the devil.

''My fiancée's brother who opposes our marriage.''

Immediately the door of the inn opened and the fiancée's brother appeared. ''Get going,'' the devil whispered in the boy's ear. ''Seize the opportunity. No one will see or hear you. Provoke him . . . say nasty things to him . . . the battle will come by itself.''

The boy rose, went up to his fiancée's brother and said something into his ear. The brother started and looked at the boy with big, questioning eyes. Then the boy spat in his face. The two men went out of the inn while the devil settled down at the window.

At the end of barely two minutes the boy came back into the inn. He was covered in dust and his clothes were spattered with blood. There was a light in the depths of his eyes and he was smiling. ''I've killed him,'' he cried, ''I've killed him and I enjoyed seeing him die!''

A brass band invaded the courtyard of the inn. A brass band of devils who were playing tunes that soldiers like.

''Let us follow the band,'' said the devil to the boy. ''Let us go to the next village and tell the peasants that you have killed their son. They will get out their guns . . . they'll try to attack you . . . your people will come and defend you. Come on, soldier, the war is waiting for us!''

The brass band, the devil and the soldier went off in the direction of the neighbouring village. And the band played fine tunes, and the devil danced, and the boy laughed . . . Then the soldier multiplied: two soldiers, then four soldiers, then eight, then sixteen, then thirty-two, then sixty-four, then a hundred and twenty-eight, then two hundred and fifty-six, then five hundred and twelve, then a thousand and twenty-four, then two thousand and forty-eight, then four thousand and ninety-six . . . There were curses, insults, then blows, then gunshots; people ran, hid, attacked, defended themselves, killed, fell down, got up, fell down again . . . The guns arrived; all sorts of guns, small ones, medium-sized ones, big ones, less small ones and bigger ones; then cannons, machine-guns, airplanes fitted with weapons, ships fitted with weapons, cars, trains, tractors, buses, fire engines, bicycles, scooters, baby carriages fitted with weapons . . . The struggle grew more and more violent, without ever stopping. It went on and on and on and on.

Then one day, when the sky was clear, the devil made a little sign with his hand and the mushroom appeared.